H

PERCY
PUBLISHING

Enquiries should be addressed to
Percy Publishing
Woodford Green,
Essex. IG8 0TF
England.
www.percy-publishing.com

1st Published January 2014
1st Edition

ISBN : 978-0-9571568-2-1

Cover Design Copyright © 2013 Percy Publishing
Percy Publishing is a Clifford Marker Associates Ltd Company

I would like to thank all the people that helped me put this book together. Ruth Killeen my Literary Agent, Cherry Burroughs for her help in dotting the i's and crossing the t's and Percy Publishing for having faith in this story.

Prologue

Chris Carter stared into own reflection as the grey-green scenery rushed past the window. He was on his own now, his parents left behind at King's Cross station. He had no idea what he had let himself in for when the tannoy announced that the train would shortly be arriving at Darlington.

***

A bushy-moustached corporal stood tall, looking down at Chris Carter, his beady eyes framed by the slashed peak of his cap.

"Name?" he barked.

"Chris!" came the answer.

"We on first name terms?" the corporal snapped. "Name?" was barked again.

Carter looked down, and was amazed at how shiny the corporal's boots were, gleaming in the fluorescent light of the station platform. "Carter," he answered meekly.

"Well Carter, get your shit together and get in the mini bus outside that entrance!

The bus in which Carter found himself sitting with eight other quietly scared young men was a Leyland Sherpa. The driver approached yet another roundabout at speed, causing all the passengers to slide from side to side as the vehicle swayed on its suspension. The indicator flashed, and they approached a red and white barrier manned by a tired-faced young man in combats. The sign behind the fence announced that this was Helles Barracks, and once inside they soon pulled up outside a red brick building. The corporal got out of the front passenger seat, pulled the side panel door open and bawled, "Get your shit together, get in those doors, and get upstairs! The corporal up there will show you your allocated rooms. Training starts tomorrow morning, so get a good night's sleep boys – and welcome to the Army!!"

***

Four weeks later standing straight-backed and proud, Carter marched up to a table positioned in the middle of the parade square. He halted in crisp military fashion, his immaculately shiny books hitting the tarmac, and gave the regulation salute: long way up – hold! - short way down.

"Number?" demanded the officer sitting there.

"24828672, Sir!"

"What does Certo Cito stand for? "

"Swift but sure, Sir!"

"Who is our Commander in Chief?"

"Her Royal Highness the Princess Royal, Princess Anne, Sir!"

"Thank you, Signaller," and the officer stood up, took a dark blue beret from the table and handed it to Carter, who placed it on his head and saluted once again.

"How are you enjoying the training, Signaller?"

"Enjoying it, Sir!"

The Troop Training Sergeant spoke up. "He is one of the better ones, Sir."

"Good to hear! Have a well-deserved weekend off, and then finish your training"

"Thank y ou, Sir!" Carter saluted again, performing a smart about turn in a perfect army regulation drill movement. Wearing the beret of the Royal Signals as he marched away from the table made him feel proud to be part of something.

***

It was April 1988; there had been rain and the air smelt clean and fresh. Carter stood in his Number Two dress, everything immaculate. His boots were like black glass, and the buckle of his belt gleamed in the snippets of sun light. He stood at the end of the troop: Two Troop. Of the thirty-eight original recruits only thirty now remained. Training had not been too hard, most men dropping out because they were home sick; a couple had been injured, or found not to be fit enough, but only two had been back-squadded.

"Form up lads, make yourselves proud! You only pass out once in your life, so make it a good one!" barked the Training Sergeant.

The first thump of the bass drum sent a quiver through Carter's heart as he stepped off with his left foot, and he found himself fighting back the tears. Just why he was becoming so emotional he couldn't understand. After all, he had a new family now, leaving his broken home far behind him.

Chapter 1

The red brick buildings of Hammersmith Barracks glowed in the sun as the bus topped the ridge of the hill: Carter felt his stomach turn over. It had been a long Friday, and now he was about to find out what 4th Armoured Division and Signal Regiment was all about. As he stared out of the window watching the buildings get bigger, he remembered the day he had been given his posting.

"Lance Corporal Carter - 4ADSR!" the small Sergeant announced.

"Christ! What'd you do wrong to get that!" gasped Peter, who was standing next to him. His own posting had been to 2 Div in York, North Yorkshire.

"They'll eat you alive there!" laughed Micky, a short, stocky ex Radio Relay operator. Before changing trades he had served two years with 4ADSR. "If you get a Radio Relay troop, they hate techies with a vengeance. Just pray you get Mike Troop. That's where all the techs keep themselves to themselves." That was four months ago, and Carter hadn't really thought much about it until today, when he saw the barracks looming up on him. They were impressive three-story blocks, surrounded by a concrete and metal fence.

The bus pulled up at the entrance, where a young soldier dressed in combats lifted a barrier and allowed them to drive in. They stopped again, and another soldier came aboard with a clip board and called out, "Carter, Harken, and Hampton!" Carter was first off, followed by two other young men both looking no older than sixteen.

A corporal, dressed in combats, now turned up, looked at the new arrivals then consulted his list. "Signaller Harken and Signaller Hampton, you're both in 2 Squadron. See that second block to the left?" He turned and pointed out a road between two blocks. "Get your stuff off the bus and then go to the main entrance there and find a Corporal Smart." He turned to Carter. "You're with me, Carter, joining 1 Squadron. We've been expecting you – Micky's already told some of the lads a bit about you!" Carter felt his stomach knot a little. He had never really got on with Micky during technical training in 8 Signal Regiment, and ten to one he'd set him up for a fall with some of his old cronies. It was supposed to be hard enough joining your first unit, without someone stirring it up before you got there.

"My name's Peter and I'm with Cheetah Troop; you're in Panther Troop. Jonah is waiting for you over in the squadron lines. The regiment stands down on a Friday lunch time, so the weekend is yours until Parade, Monday morning at eight. Get your stuff and head over to that block over there." He pointed to a block behind the building where they were standing.

Even though it was only early April, it was a warm day and Carter was conscious of the heat of the mid afternoon sun. Finding his green sausage bag and green holdall already unloaded from the coach by the driver, he slung the heavy bag over his shoulder, picked up the holdall and made his way to the block Peter had pointed out. Above the entrance was written *1 SQUADRON*, and as he walked through the double doors into the foyer he noticed how shiny the floor was. To the front were stairs leading upwards; to both left and right a set of glass and wooden doors. "Hello!" Carter called out. "Hello, Jonah!" he called again. Above him he could hear footsteps clumping down the stairs, and then suddenly a tall, very handsome, blonde man of about twenty four appeared on the top step. He looked like the perfect Aryan of Hitler's ideal world, standing at the top of the staircase in what had been the barracks of one of the Fuhrer's crack tank regiments. Jonah could have been a ghost from the past.

"Carter is it?" he said with a Birmingham drawl. "Been expecting you - so have some of the boys. Micky's been stirring it up for you a bit." Carter sighed. He'd known this was going to be hard, but he would have liked it on equal terms, without someone else getting their oar in first. "Don't worry about it! Most of the boys are out down the town. Payday this week, so they're off blowing the lot," Jonah smiled and motioned him to follow, adding, "I'll show you your room." Carter picked up his bags. "We're on the top floor." Jonah called back. "I'm the highest rank and most senior, so I'm the Lines NCO."

The top floor turned out to have the same layout as on the ground floor, with a set of double doors each side of the corridor. Above one set it read *Cheetah Troop Lines* and above the other *Panther Troop Lines.* "This is your new home for the next few years!" and Jonah opened the door to Panther Troop Lines. The first thing to catch Carter's attention was the carpet, which was a bright emerald green. "Door to the left leads to ablutions: we have showers, bath and a drying room. The door to the right leads to the washing machines and the kitchen, though we're not allowed anything *in* the kitchen, in case we burn the place down or injure ourselves!" Jonah laughed at some joke Carter obviously had not understood.

"These are regimental orders, guard rosters and any other bits of information you need to know." Jonah pointed at a green felt board, but Carter's eyes were glued to the board beside it, which was covered in photos and what looked like letters. Jonah smiled. "That's the Pigs' Board. Do you have a girlfriend back at home?"

"Yes."

"Well, I give it three months before you get a Dear John. She'll be shagging someone else before you know it."

Looking at Jonah, Carter could see that what he'd just said in such a matter of fact way was no joke. "Look, you're nineteen; she must be about the same. You're now in a regiment that's on exercise nine months a year, and if you're lucky you get to go home Christmas, Easter and in the summer. She's not going to see you for months, and all her mates will be having a laugh. Do think she'll miss out waiting for you?"

Carter looked a bit more closely at the board, with its pictures of girls in differing states of dress. Some were of girls with nice smiles in pretty dresses, and some were of slightly uncomfortable looking girls showing off their breasts, with a couple of pictures of what looked like girls carrying out sex acts. Jonah smiled. "Some of the boys try and outdo each other with the pictures - the Sergeant Major told me to get a few of the more OTT ones taken off." They moved on through another set of double doors. "Your room's on the right. You're sharing with Toz, Mark and Lenny. This is my room here. I have a single room and so does Barker."

Carter looked around his new home. There were four single beds with a locker to the side of each one. It was no different to the layout in the training camps he had just come from: single bed and locker. The only difference here was carpet, and not tiled floors needing to be kept polished at all times.

"That's your bed in the corner. Settle yourself in, and I'll come and get you at four thirty and show you where the canteen is." Jonah left the room, shutting the door behind him.

***

Carter looked around him. The room was every bit as basic as he had been used to at the Technical School of 8 Signal Regiment in Catterick. The lockers were the same military issue: one side with a rail for hanging clothes, and the other made of cubby holes for storing various things. If you were in training, your uniform would use up the entire locker in regulation layout. Between each locker was a single bed with a green plastic mattress.

The other beds here had been individualized with quilts of wildly varying designs. One was emblazoned with the image of the Trap Door, a popular children's plasticine animation programme; another with a model on a beach, and yet another displayed the Scottish flag. Above the beds were various pictures, posters and mementos. There was a used ticket to a Rangers/ Celtic game in Glasgow; there was a picture of a wedding, one of a young girl in school uniform, and another of what looked like parents. These were the keepsakes of his new roommates. Carter couldn't begin to guess what his new colleagues were going to be like.

He began to unpack his things.

***

Once unpacked, he went to the bathroom. He was surprised to be met by the sight of a row of urinals, and behind them another row, this time of cubicle toilets. Sticking out of the tiled wall were eight shower heads with no separation, and there was one bath within the same style cubicle as the toilets. This was not Five Star: this was No Star At All. Carter could feel his heart sink as he looked about him, mentally saying goodbye to any vestiges of the relative comfort of his old life. So this was what he had signed up for! He'd expected the facilities to be bad during training, but had been confident that when he got to his first Unit all that would change. He had pictured himself living a dignified existence with colleagues, probably in a self-contained flat, not as part of some pack. In the back of his mind he could hear his friends warning him about joining the Army.

Now, as he looked around, he wondered if it had indeed been a bad mistake.

***

Lying on his bed with its regulation two sheets and a blanket, and scanning the room for the umpteenth time, Carter decided he was going out tomorrow to buy a duvet. Above each of the lockers were packed Bergen's and webbing belts; on the shelves to the side of them were ash trays. Not being a smoker, this was something he loathed about the army. In a place where you were supposed to keep fit about 90% of the men smoked. He hated it! - had hated it as a child when his dad used to smoke in the family car. Now it looked like all three of the others smoked and smoked in this room.

There was a sharp knock and Jonah was standing in the doorway. "You want to know where to get some grub?"

He jumped up off his bed, glad of something to do at last. "Love some, I'm starving!" and he followed Jonah out of the room.

As they left the block the heat hit Carter, who hadn't realised how cool the rooms inside had been. The sky was a turquoise blue, the late afternoon sun beginning to sink lower towards the horizon. The cook house turned out to be in a building identical to the living quarters, but this time the double entrance doors led into an open area furnished with dining tables and plastic chairs. To their left as they walked in was a long row of stainless steel catering hot plates, with heat lamps keeping the food warm.

Carter followed Jonah to where the hotplates started and they collected plastic trays, plates and cutlery.

Placing the trays on the runner, they worked their way down a selection of burgers, sausages, lasagne, chips, mash, greens and gravy looking no better than your average school dinner.

"This is it, don't get any better! Cook house is empty first weekend of the month - the boys are out blowing their wages on proper food, beer and women. Come Wednesday they'll all be skint and back in here moaning about how shit this food is," Jonah smiled. Carter just nodded and followed. Once past the meat and veg, they came to the desserts. Treacle pudding, spotted dick, coconut slices. Jonah took a chunk of spotted dick and covered it in a generous helping of custard. Carter chose the coconut slice with custard.

Making his way to the second row of tables, Jonah sat down and Carter sat opposite. Jonah got up and asked if he wanted some juice before going over to a table with two urns on it and a container full of orange juice. Jonah handed one of the glasses of orange over to Carter and looked down at his food. "Shit! Always *is* shit," he moaned. "We get better scran when we're on exercise, though, which is lucky because we're out of Camp nine months of the year." Jonah pushed his food around the plate a bit, before scooping some on a fork and eating it. Carter looked stonily at his own food: it wasn't that good but not that bad either. He didn't say anything, just began to eat in silence.

"So what's your story?" Jonah asked.

"What do you mean?"

"Why are you here, why the Army?"

"Parents split up; Dad earned too much for me to get a university grant, so he talked me into getting a trade and life experience in the Army. He's ex- Royal Engineers himself."

"What do you think so far?"

"It's not what I expected. Basic and tech training was very easy - have no idea what it's going to be like here."

"Clever guy like you. Shit! The best thing you can do is get the fuck out of here as soon as, before the place drags you down."

Carter didn't know what to say, so just kept quiet.

"The lads here are fucking animals. They got asked to name the junior ranks' Mess Bar. Could have called it anything they wanted. They called it the 'Pigs' Bar.' Need I say anything else? So," he went on, "you've got a girlfriend back home then!"

"Yeah, been seeing her for a couple of years."

"My advice is, forget her, here and now at this table, and get stuck into the local populace." Jonah looked serious. "I am not joking! Like I said earlier, you're nineteen. She'll have all the lads sniffing round her, and her mates will be out having fun. You'll be on exercise weeks at a time with no contact, and she'll be getting entertained by some kind hearted soul within weeks, mate. Guaranteed!"

Carter didn't feel like arguing the defence, and by now they'd both nearly finished their meal.

"Look Carter, you've got nothing to do until Monday morning. Come down the town with me tonight and let's see how we get on. Do you like running?"

"Yes," Carter answered. In fact he'd found army training so easy because he could run and walk for miles, and had been able to since he was a young child.

"Let's go out tonight and have some fun then, and I'll

take you on some of the running circuits around here tomorrow morning."

Chapter 2

The music filled his head and he could feel his body vibrating to the beat. Carter stood at a bar to the side of a massive dance floor lit by colourful flashing lights, smoke wafting up around the undulating dancers. Jonah walked over with two bottles of Hereforder beer and passed one to Carter, who thanked him by tapping the bottle against Jonah's. "Do it properly, man!" Jonah tapped his bottle hard on top of Carter's. "Now you on mine!" Carter did so, and then raised the bottle to his mouth just as it frothed over, making him step back sharply before it spilled all down his shirt. Jonah laughed out loud. "Muppet!!" he shouted in delight. "You'll have to watch out with the lads if you can be caught out that easy – they'll eat you alive!

Take a look at the talent in here. If they speak English to you, you're in! You'll need to learn a bit of German to open the conversation, but they know you're a squaddie and all they want is a bit of fun with you. These German birds are not like the girls back home. They'll suck your cock as easy as having a goodnight kiss. They're brought up a bit different over here when it comes to sex."

Carter looked around at the girls dressed for a night out, hair all sprayed, and he noticed a lot of glances at both him and Jonah as they passed. "With your dark hair and my blond," Jonah went on, "we make a good team!" He looked Carter up and down, adding, "The birds here like it one way or the other."

Carter finished his beer. "How do you ask for a beer then?"

"Eins Beer bitte for one, Zwei Beer bitte for two. You need to learn your numbers, and I'll go through some other basic German with you tomorrow. You *could* sign up for a course, but the best thing is to get a German girl to teach you. More fun that way!" Jonah winked.

Carter turned to the bar and motioned to the barmaid for two beers. She smiled at him and Carter smiled back, looking at her figure as she bent down to get the bottles from the chiller. He didn't really have it in his mind to sleep with anyone behind his girlfriend's back – he never had done in their two year relationship, nor ever felt the need to. He wondered what she was doing now: was she clubbing with her university mates, or in her room studying hard for her chemistry degree.

"Who then is this?" Carter heard a German voice ask in Pidgin English.

"This is Chris Carter. Flew in today." Jonah motioned to a dark, wide-eyed girl. "His first day here. Still trying to find his feet."

"'ello! My name is Helga."

"Hello Helga, my name is Chris. Nice to meet you!" Carter answered, looking her up and down. She was about 5'6", slim but with an ample cleavage, which she enhanced with a tight silky dress just above the knee. "Would you like a drink?" he asked.

Helga smiled and moved to Carter's side, rubbing her

body against his. Looking up into his eyes, she murmured huskily, "Would love one, soldier boy!"

He could feel his penis begin to harden in his trousers as this girl's eyes seemed to swallow him up, and was taken aback at finding himself so easily aroused by the way she was playing him. Jonah tapped him on the shoulder. "She'll chew you up and spit you out! She likes to have all the new blood."

"Another beer?" Carter asked, and Jonah nodded. "And what would you like, Helga?"

"Brandy and lemonade - and one for my friend too?"

"Of course. What will she have?"

"Same!"

Jonah was towering like a giant over a young blonde, and winked at Carter as he noticed him looking.

"So, how do you like it here?" asked Helga.

"What?" Carter answered distractedly.

"How do you like it here?" she repeated.

Carter looked at his watch. "Been here a total of five hours. Got into barracks about four."

"What barracks you at?"

"Don't know the name - 4ADSR"

"Oh - with Jonah on Limenska Strasse"

"Yeah." Carter turned and paid for the drinks, then handed one of the brandy and lemonades to Helga and the other to Jonah, as the blonde girl still had her back to him.

"Thank you, Chris!" Helga seemed to purr as she took a sip of the drink. "Do you want to dance?"

Carter shook his head. "I don't dance."

"I will dance, and you just move and watch me!" Helga grabbed his hand and steered him to the dance floor,

21

passing Jonah, who now was kissing the faceless girl that had joined them.

***

By now Carter's head was swimming. The dance floor was a blur, the heat was making him light headed, and he could taste the dry ice smoke at the back of his throat. Helga was gyrating in front of him, teasing him with her moves, teasing those around her with her body. A number of times he had seen her push away men who seemed more than ready to join her. Carter had stood to the side with a bottle of beer in his hand, moving a bit but mostly just watching Helga, and occasionally leaving the dance floor to replenish his beer. Jonah had seated himself on a bar stool, and the last time Carter had gone to the bar he had seen that the girl he was with was standing between his legs rubbing his crotch. Jonah had smiled and pulled the girl's head to his lips by her hair, saying to Carter as he went by, "they like it rough, these girls here. No idea who this one is, but she wants it bad!" Carter could see he was drunk and the girl, who seemed just as drunk, gave him a dumb, glassy-eyed smile as he passed Jonah another beer.

He made his way back onto the crowded dance floor to find Helga now rubbing up and down on some guy to the thudding beat of the Theme from S-Express. When she saw Carter she smiled and worked her way up to him, moving her body to the music like a serpent. "Dancing makes me so horny, Carter!" she whispered as she guided his earlobe into her mouth. Carter felt goose bumps all over his body. "Do you want me to suck you cock?" she breathed.

"What!" Carter couldn't believe his ears.

"I want to suck you cock until you cum in my mouth," Helga purred. "I am so horny I want your cock in my mouth."

"I don't even know you!" Carter blurted out. He couldn't believe his ears. He had seen this sort of thing on porn films he had watched with his mates, but this! – he didn't believe this really happened.

"Do you not like your cock being sucked?" Helga asked. "I bet you have a nice thick cock that will make me gag. I bet you will thrust it into my throat when you cum. I want to taste your cum!" Carter looked into the eyes of this girl he had only just met. She was a pretty girl with a nice figure and lovely deep brown eyes. He could not understand why she would act like this.

"Come with me!" Helga grabbed his arm and pulled him off the dance floor into a corridor that led to the exit. Once outside, with the neon lights of the club lighting the way, Helga led Carter first to the right, then down a road to a brightly illuminated underpass. It was empty but looked well used, as it was clean and properly maintained. She stopped a little way into the underpass and leant against the wall. Then she grabbed the back of Carter's neck and pulled him close, kissing him, opening her mouth and exploring his with her soft wet tongue. At the same time, Carter could feel one of her hands working to undo his belt, and her warm hand was suddenly on his penis, rubbing up and down. "I knew you would have a nice cock!" she sighed.

Carter looked both ways along the underpass as Helga dropped to her knees. "What if someone comes?"

"They get to see me suck your cock," she said, as she began using her tongue on the end of Carter's penis. Fuck! he thought, so what if someone sees us! She doesn't seem bothered. He felt her take his penis in her warm, moist mouth, which she started to work up and down his shaft. Her hands were on his testicles massaging his balls as she moaned, and he felt her middle finger begin teasing his anus. He was now fully charged and thrusting his hips, then suddenly he was past the point of return and felt the build as he released his cum, pushing his penis deep into her mouth.

Once he had cum, Helga spent some time licking his penis. When she stood up Carter pulled her thighs apart and felt the wetness between her legs. "I want to fuck you!" he growled.

"NO! I only fuck my husband!"

"What?" Carter asked, hot and wanting to get between her legs.

"I only fuck my husband. I like to suck cock, but I don't fuck."

"What now, then?"

"You go back to your mate and find a girl. I go home and fuck my husband if he wants me."

Carter looked at Helga for a moment as she stood there. Then he turned and made his way back to the club alone.

***

Jonah was getting more and more turned on by the blonde. She hadn't really said much, except that she was nineteen and called Julia. She was pissed now, and he knew he was going to fuck her.

"Who's the handsome devil you were with earlier?" a voice asked over his shoulder.

"Oh, hi Ingrid! How come you're here! Where's Staff Green? Thought he didn't let you out!"

"On another fucking course. Six week drill course in Pirbright. Wouldn't take me and Jimmy because Jimmy's just started nursery school."

"Who you with then?"

"Couple of the girls, just having a blowout. Suzie and Tracey's husbands both on stag, so we thought we'd come out."

"Don't do anything I would!" Jonah smiled. He'd always liked Ingrid; had no idea how a guy like Green got a girl as good as this. He was an ugly, short-arsed redhead, and even though he kept himself very fit, he still looked plump.

"Nice looking lad. You want to introduce me?" Ingrid asked. Jonah looked at her slightly glassy eyes and decided that would not be the best thing to do at all.

"I think he's gone off with one of the locals." Jonah motioned around, as if Carter had gone. "Me and Julia are leaving now too."

"Shame! - I'd have liked to have met him."

Jonah looked at Ingrid. This was a bit unusual for her: one, to be out; second to pay any attention to a new boy in the regiment. She was always so much under the thumb of Staff Green, and when he was around no one was allowed even so much as to look at her. "We're off now then, Ingrid," he said. "Have a quiet night!"

She watched Jonah go, and then looked around the dance floor for the new guy again, before being heckled by her two friends to join them at the bar.

Chapter 3

Carter had found his rhythm, his breathing now in sync with his legs as he glided along the road at a steady pace. To his right Jonah was running with the same ease. They had left the barracks a few minutes ago and were just coming to the outskirts of a housing estate. The path cut between two houses before turning into a gravel track leading into a wood.

"What happened last night?" Jonah asked. "I heard a bit of a palaver in the corridor when you came in."

"Mark was sleeping on the floor outside the room when I got back, then gave me a load of shit about locking the door. Allegedly, they don't lock it when they go out. 'Only a cunt would lock the door '- his words."

"Don't worry about Mark. He's a funny fucker: not good on his drink, gets aggressive. Even though he's short, he grows a foot taller and a foot wider for every pint he drinks. He'd have been pissed, and the boys would have sent him home."

"Nice way to meet one of my new roommates!" Carter moaned.

"Don't worry about it! He'll get over it, though he is a moody fucker."

Carter thought back to last night. He'd gone back to the club to find Jonah, but looking round the bar, he was nowhere to be seen, so he'd decided to call it a night. He made his way to the taxi rank and asked the driver to take him to the barracks; luckily the driver had spoken English and got him there without any dramas, the bored gate guard letting him in without comment.

When he got to his room there was body sleeping outside with his coat rolled up as a pillow, and as he unlocked the door there was torrid of abuse in strong Glaswegian that Carter had difficulty understanding. This was followed up by the threat of a beating before the guy stood by his bed, stripped off and climbed in. Then within what seemed like seconds, he was snoring quietly!

Carter had gone to the bathroom to clean his teeth and wash his face. As he passed Jonah's room he heard a high pitch squeal and the rhythm of bed springs.

Lying in bed later, he tried to assess his first day as a soldier serving in a British Army unit in Germany. It could not *really* be like this! This was not what the posters had depicted, and when he joined as an electronics technician he thought he would be doing something clever, worthwhile, interesting.

The wooded path now began to rise steeply into a ridge. Carter did not slow down and he could see Jonah was beginning to increase the pace, so he increased his too – keeping Jonah at his side.

"What happened to the girl you brought back last night?"

"Left her in my room when we came out. Either she'll still be there when I get back, or she's made her way home. Not my concern! If she *is* there, I'll give her another go. If not, then we'll go and grab some lunch in the canteen"

"What's your plan for tonight?"

"Same as last night. Go to a club and see what's about. There's nothing else to do around here. You can stay in and watch a video, read a book or go out pulling birds. Depends what takes your fancy. Don't go out with Toz or Lenny, though! They're animals, and you don't want to get into their idea of fun. Beer, fag and a fight is their idea of a night out. They don't go chasing girls unless they can get one who'll sleep with the both of them at the same time. They stick to each other like glue. If they weren't such mentals you'd think they were gay. Sorry to say, they're both your room mates!"

What with Mark last night, and now finding out he had two other unstable roommates, Carter was not getting a warm fuzzy feeling about his new home. The path had become a steep set of terraces leading directly up the ridge for about six hundred metres. Despite running now for about half an hour, Carter had not lost any of his stride, and Jonah hadn't broken into a sweat either. Jonah opened his stride again pushing hard up the hill. Carter repeated the pace step for step.

"What plans you got for your career?" asked Jonah.

"Have none - don't know much about it. Just got told that, as a technician, I should be a Sergeant in five years. Don't really know anything about the Army. Don't know if I like it, to be truthful."

"Well, if you don't know if you like the army you're in the shittiest place in the world. We're on exercise all the time, and the lads are all a bit green, mad, pissed off or suicidal. You'll have to learn to go one way or the other! I've been here four years. Made full screw, which is good for a radio relay operator. Been trying to get out here for two years. Applied for 264, but they have no requirements for operators at the moment. I'm waiting for my starting date with 13 Intelligence, but that's already taken a year to come through." Jonah was talking as he paced himself up the hill.

"This place is boring as hell. Unless you're a Green mad soldier, this place will get to you. Try and get out as soon as you can. Ley has volunteered for every volunteer regiment in the UK and still can't get out of here. He wants to get a UK posting so he can see his girlfriend. 264, 216 and the Marine Detachment – he's done all the courses, and passed the fitness side of it but fails the technical bit. 216 Para would have had him but they have no technician openings, and he wouldn't re-trade to a radio operator to get in."

"I'll just play it as it goes," responded Carter.

"Well, I'm telling you, if you don't have a game plan to get out of here, this place will swallow you up!"

***

They got back to the barracks after running for an hour and a half. Stretching off outside the block Jonah stated that Carter would do OK with the phys there. If he could keep up a good pace on a run and carry weight, then there would be no worries about physical training. "The phys in this place isn't too hard, if you're fit."

They made their way to their rooms. "You think she's still in there?" Carter motioned to Jonah's door.

"Let's have a look!" Jonah swung his door open to reveal a mop of blonde hair poking above the bed covers. "Yes, she still is. I'll see you later, Carter!"

Carter went to his room, where Mark was still snoring in his bed. He looked at the clock: it was eleven thirty. Carter was not a sleeper and couldn't sleep past six in the morning, let alone sleep the morning away. Keeping as quiet as he could, he found his towel and wash gear and headed for the shower.

Chapter 4

When he got back to their room Mark was lying on his bed with a cigarette hanging from his lips. Red-eyed and pasty-faced, he watched Carter put his wash kit into his locker and get some clean clothes out. The idea of Mark silently watching him like that, as lf inspecting him, was unnerving, and he felt uncomfortable as he dropped his towel to get changed, putting on his boxer shorts as quickly as he could.

"Don't lock the fucking door again, you cunt!" growled Mark as soon as Carter had his boxers on. Carter didn't know how to respond to this, so stayed silent as he pulled his jeans on, and then pulled his t-shirt over his head. "Oi, Cunt! I'm talking to you!" Mark growled again.

Carter turned to look at Mark who was still lying in his bed. "What's the issue? I thought it natural to lock the door," he said, "By the way, my name's Chris."

"I know who the fuck you are. We get told when we have new roommates. You're the new baby tech tosser." Mark's eyes narrowed. "Was the door locked when you got here?"

Carter had assumed the door was not locked because he was a new arrival. "No!"

"That's 'cause we all lost our keys, and we are not going to pay for new ones. So in the future leave the fucking door open!"

"Hey mate, what's with the aggression? I've only just turned up, and you're being a bit off!"

"*Aggression?*, a *bit off!*" Mark jeered. "You some sort of toff? I cannot believe it! - we now have a poncy southern twat in the room!"

Carter had never come across this sort of behaviour before, and had no idea how to handle it. This guy had made up his mind not to like him before he had even arrived. He didn't know whether he should go out for the morning, then come back and see if the situation had calmed down, or stay and ride it out.

As he was contemplating going for a long walk, the door opened and two young lads came in. "Mark, you tosser! Where the fuck did you end up last night?" the short, stocky one asked.

"Yeah, mate! It was your fucking round, and you just upped and fucked off!" chipped in the other one, a tall and lanky lad.

"Piss off! I was too pissed to do anything, and I just wanted my bed."

"Should've stayed. The little one that Toz was chatting too was a right little lady and when we got back to hers she had a flat mate that was so pissed she had no idea what Lenny was doing."

"Yeah man, she was pretty passed out; was still passed out when I left this morning. I think she may have a shock when she wakes up!" Lenny grinned.

"Yeah, you weird bastard! Kept wanting to cum on her face as she slept. Must have done it three times."

Lenny just smiled. "Left it to dry so it was there when

she woke up."

"Weirdo!" Toz laughed.

"I couldn't be arsed with that bird *you* were talking to. She was too fat and had hair on her face," Mark jeered.

"And you're an oil painting? You short-arsed Jock twat!" Toz retorted. Then he turned to Carter. "So you're the new baby tech then. Welcome to 4 Div, the shittiest div of the Corps! What did you do wrong to get this posting?"

"Hello!" Carter walked over to offer a handshake.

"You a fag or something, you want to touch me!" Toz laughed, ignoring Carter's hand. "We already been told about you - bit of a ponce is what I hear. That's what Micky told us. Bit of a flash git. Well, you won't get to be too flash here!"

Carter's stomach rolled over. What the fuck was wrong with this place! It was like he was having a nightmare, and he just wanted to wake up. What had Micky said, and why? He'd never really had much to do with him in training.

"And don't think that stripe means anything here! *You* get them when you finish your training, I had to earn mine. Three years here to get my first stripe: you get yours for passing your classroom exams."

Carter knew about the other trades' resentment of a technician's promotion. The Royal Corps of Signals is made up of various trades, from radio operators to technicians, who all have different roles to play. Technicians go through twelve months technical training and exams to be awarded their position. When trained and in their units, they are responsible for maintaining equipment and ensuring it works.

During training they have to pass various mathematics and engineering exams. The career path is to be promoted to Sergeant within five years and the pay is one of the highest in the military for junior ranks. After the training they are made Lance Corporal, and within two years Corporal, after the successful completion of another exam. Then they have to go back to Catterick for a T1 course, which is another year's technical training, before becoming a Sergeant. Once in a Regiment, they have no special privileges and have to live and work with the other ranks and trades.

Sharing a room of four with other soldiers who might resent him was never going to be easy. Back in training he had heard nightmare stories, and now it looked like he was about to start living one. Carter knew he had only one way out of this, which was to win these lads over, but he had no idea of the best way to deal with Toz, so he just kept quiet.

"I am the senior in this room so," Toz paused for effect, "you stay to your bit of it and keep it tidy. The TV and hi-fi are ours, so don't think of touching them." Carter started to make a move for the door. "Oh, and don't come back for a couple of hours. I need some sleep"

Lenny, who stood by Toz's side, just kept quiet with his eyes fixed on Carter, who tried not to smile: Lenny had one of those looks about him suggesting that his eyes and brain were not quite linked together.

Toz moved over to his bed, took a packet of cigarettes from his pocket, pulled one out and lit it. "Do you smoke, Carter?"

"No."

"Unlucky! We all smoke in here," he jeered.

Carter went out of the room, leaving the three lads behind him. This was surreal, a nightmare, and definitely not what he had expected when he first walked into the Army Recruiting Office. It had all looked like an adventure, with him as a professional soldier off to live the life of an adventurer. Everyone fit, clean, tough, knowing their job and being part of a team - being the best, that's what they sold him: be the best, be a soldier in the British Army, be part of a team!

So far he had experienced easy training, with mismatched human beings who all seemed to have an "issue" of some sort, or were running away from something. How many had dropped out from training! How many had not been able to run more than a mile when they first arrived! How different it all was from the future he'd been looking forward to when he repeated the oath and took his ten pounds for joining. He wanted desperately to speak to Jonah, to see if Jonah could help him - talk to Toz, tell him everything was OK. 'Toz, Carter's a good lad, he's one of us! Micky was just pulling your chain!" But he was reluctant to knock on the closed door. Jonah was probably still entertaining the girl he had in his room.

As Carter walked out of the block, the spring morning sun hit him. It was brilliantly bright, more warm than crisp. He looked up to the sky, glad to be breathing in the air. All around him were numerous three storey blocks; to his right he could see the perimeter wall, topped with barbed wire, the sound of traffic coming from behind it. Carter decided to go for a walk into this new town which was to be his home for the next few years. Two bored looking soldiers in camouflage combat suits stood at the gate of the barracks entrance, both armed with SLR rifles. Neither of them spoke, or indeed paid him any attention as he passed them on his way out.

At the road he turned left and headed towards Herford Town Centre, looking at the buildings around him as he went. They were all pretty much the same: cream coloured and solid, with shuttered windows. A lot of the cars driving along the road were Mercedes Benz and BMWs. Compared to England the cars all looked quite expensive, and he was surprised to see that even the taxis were cream coloured Mercs. He was used to mini cabs in England - beat up rust buckets of any make, but mainly Japanese.

As he went he kept his eyes out for a little shop where he could buy something to drink. His throat was dry, he could feel his stomach cramping, and his head was beginning to ache. His mind was still full of what had just happened in the room, and he wanted to forget it: to walk, relax, go back and find it had all been a wind up, a joke; that they were just pulling his chain. Carter smiled at the thought. *Was* it just a wind up? Had he fallen for it? Would he get back to the room and find Jonah there with Mark, Toz and Lenny taking the piss out of him? This thought cheered him up as he walked. Arriving at last in the town centre he found a little shop, empty apart from a large man behind the counter who sported a bushy grey moustache. Carter smiled to himself, wondering at what stage in their life would someone think, 'I know what my face needs, a big bushy moustache. That'll attract the girls, and make me look important!" On scanning the shelves, he didn't recognise a lot of the items and even some of those that *were* recognisable had different names, like Marathon Bar, which was called 'Snickers'. He went to the fridge and took out a can of Fanta, and decided on a 'Snickers' bar to see if it really was the same as a 'Marathon.' When he went to pay for his items the man asked him for a figure in German that he didn't understand. Reaching into his pocket, he pulled out some coins and put them on the counter, letting the big man take what he needed. Then he simply swept up the change and nodded pleasantly, hearing the shop keeper call out 'Tag!' as he left.

Once outside, Carter sat on a wall, opened the can, and took a bite of the 'Snickers/Marathon' bar. The sickly sweetness tasted reassuringly the same! Sitting there, letting the world pass by, he began to think of his roommates again. They seemed an odd lot. Toz, the "leader", was a short stocky lad with a lazy eye, mousy brown hair, and the scar from a hare lip. Shit! He didn't have much going for him. No wonder he was a bit aggressive. Then there was Lenny: tall, lanky, gormless- looking and talked with a drawl; obviously under Toz's command. Mark seemed and looked normal in comparison, but he too was clearly very much under the influence of Toz. He was about five-six, with unremarkable features, short dark hair and blue eyes.

Where was this going to end? Was it a wind up? Would he turn out to be like one of the victims of 'Beadles About' - all embarrassed and humble pie when the lads explained they did the same to everyone when they first arrived! The door was all a joke. Of course they locked it: be stupid not to. He'd been told 4 Div was a hard regiment, but he thought the stories were probably a bit exaggerated. There was talk of a lot of AWOLs, just doing a runner from the Army, and 4 Div had a reputation for bullying and fighting. The Junior Ranks' Bar was called the 'Pigs' Bar' because they were supposed to be proud to be pigs, living in their own wallow. If any of this was true, what did the senior soldiers think, and why weren't the officers doing anything about it?

Should he go back to his room now, take the wind-up on the chin, smile and then start to get to know his roommates? Bond, get to be lifelong buddies, comrades in arms like in the movies! Carter looked at his watch. He had only been out of his room for thirty five minutes, and Toz had said he wanted some sleep, so he decided to stay out until early afternoon.

When Carter got back to the door of his room he could hear it was full of activity; the TV was on and the lads were laughing. By now he'd been out for a few hours. After finding his way to the town centre he had walked the length of the High Street and into the town square, stopping at the bridge over a small river to watch some ducks. On the way back he bought himself a Hawaiian Burger- something he'd never had before, and he certainly couldn't recall the option of pineapple with his burger in England. This was followed up with some spaghetti ice cream, another dish that was alien to him. He had enjoyed sitting at a pavement table watching people pass by. The language was totally alien to him, but if he was going to be here for four years he wanted to learn some of it.

After eating his food he had made the slow walk back

to the barracks. One of the soldiers on the gate, both looking as bored as the two they had replaced, asked for his ID card. Carter was expecting some sort of conversation when he showed it, but all he got was, "New here?" which he had answered with a 'Yes." The soldier just nodded and left it at that.

When Carter walked in, the room was full of cigarette smoke. Lenny was on his bed, propped up by a pillow, Toz sat on the end of his bed, and on the sofa facing the TV were Mark and a young girl. Each of them had a bottle of beer. On the TV a detective was telling Danny Glover he was about to break in a new partner on loan from dope, some real burn out, on the ragged edge.

"If you want to watch it, you got to pay up!" Toz growled.

Having convinced himself that what happened earlier was a wind up, Carter's heart sank. He had fully expected to walk into a laughing welcoming party, all joking about what his face was like when they were giving him a hard time: what a laugh, he really did fall for it! He turned to Toz, "that's fine, how much?

"You want to stay and watch the film, that's five Ds, and you'll have to go to the Naafi and get a Herfy Handbag," Toz more sneered than growled. "If you don't, you'll have to fuck off out the room till we've watched our movie. You ain't getting the show for free!"

The young girl, who couldn't have been much more than sixteen, let out a cackle of laughter. She was short and podgy, with mousy, shoulder length hair, and wore a tight t-shirt emblazoned with the album cover of Duran Duran's Rio. Her fat breasts bulged beneath it, with the outline of her bra showing through. She was not a pretty girl, with fat lips and small eyes set too close together in her shapeless face. Mark had one arm lying lazily across her plump shoulders.

"Fine," responded Carter. "Anything else you want when I go and get some beers?"

"Fags!" the girl called out. "Get some more fags!"

"Yeah, get Emma here some fags! She never has any. Always comes up the block to ponce fags and beers," Toz put in.

"But she always pays for them," Mark grinned.

Emma slapped his leg. "Oi!"

"OK, what brand?" Carter asked,

"*OK, what brand?*" Toz mimicked Carter. "You *are* a toff! What brand? Embassy Number One, you toff. Best get sixty."

"And I'll have some Coke," Lenny called from his bed. When Carter passed Jonah's door it was still closed, but with no sounds of life behind it. Again he was tempted to knock, but instead went on past and headed for the Naafi.

The Naafi shop was in the block opposite the one Carter lived in. As well as the shop, this building housed the Pigs' Bar on the first floor, and on the second the Corporals' Mess and the Function room. Entering through a little turnstile, he was met by a shop stocked like any corner shop you would have in England. There were newspapers, paperbacks, CD's, tapes, and anything you might want to buy for day to day living Here and there amongst the familiar items was the occasional foreign product , such as German sweets, drinks and washing powder.

There was also all the usual beer you could get in the UK: Tennents cans with the girls on them; Harp, and Castlemaine XXXX. The largest pile was the Herforder Pils, in its yellow box cases with handles that the lads had nicknamed Herfy handbags. It was also the cheapest beer there. A box of ten bottles cost five Deutsche Marks. Carter picked up two, thinking he might as well take more than one back. On his way to the counter he passed a display of videos for rent at one Deutsche mark each. Carter smiled despite himself. It was costing him five Marks to watch a film he had already seen half a dozen times, and they were already part way into it! He also bought four packets of cigarettes for ten DMs. Sixty pence each – that couldn't be right!

Back in the room, Carter handed over the beer and the cigarettes. Toz held onto three packets and threw the other one over to Emma. "Here you go, my lovely!"

"Cheers, Toz!" Emma cooed.

Carter ignored her and sat on the end of his bed. On the screen Mel Gibson and Danny Glover were sitting on the back of a boat. Toz grabbed another beer and asked Carter if he wanted one, chucking a bottle in his direction. Mark opened his first, and then threw over the church key. On the sofa he could see Emma becoming the worse for wear, her head lolling onto Mark's shoulder as soon as he settled back down to drink his beer. Carter just sat quietly on his bed as the film wound to its conclusion, with Mark and Lenny giving a running commentary.

"It's not *that* fucking hard to shoot that distance with the right rifle and a good sight!"

"It is with the wind speed."

'Not if you have the right calibre. Punches through the air!'

'That's gotta hurt!'

'That's one thing I couldn't stand, getting my balls fucked up. Fingers, ribs - anything but my fucking balls. Hear about that guy in 16 Sigs with the plastic bollock?'

'Just head but him, and rip his fucking throat open!'

And so it went on and on.

As soon as the film finished and began running its credits Mark got up, stopped the video and began the rewind. "Fucking great that film! But these US Special Forces are all a bunch of pansies. They're no better than one of our shit regiments. Mate of mine did some training with some Green Berets and he got all his team in on a run before the first Yank." He went over to the hi-fi and put on some music. " Here you go, Emma! Duran Duran, just for you." Emma smiled from the sofa, her cheeks rosy from the drink and eyes slightly glassy.

Carter sat quietly on his bed; apparently forgotten by the others in the room. The interest seemed to have switched to Emma now, with Mark's lazy hand becoming more active, and Emma pushing it lethargically away. Mark gave her a kiss on the cheek. "Come on Emma, it's show time! You've had your beer, had your fags and watched your film. Now it's your time to pay." He leant across further, and pulled up the bottom of her t-shirt. She lifted her arms to let him drag it over her head, and then passively lowered them again when he reached around her, un-clasped her bra and pulled it away from her breasts. There was no smile on her face, no expression at all as she stood and took off her jeans and knickers.

Lying on his bed, Carter closed his eyes as if he was asleep. He could hear the sound of Emma's moaning, and then heard Toz call Lenny over to the sofa.

"That's it Emma baby, sit on his cock Emma! Lenny, get your cock in her mouth from there."

Carter didn't know how to react to what was going on. He could only stay quiet, not move, ignore them.

"That's it Mark, pull that arse apart! Now Emma, relax! You know how you like this cock of mine in your arse"

He just lay on his bed, eyes shut, motionless, not wanting any part of this.

Chapter 5

It was cold. Carter stood in the third row of the squad outside the Accommodation Block, about three columns away from Jonah. The troop was made up of twenty-four men, all dressed in light green fatigues, the toe caps of their boots gleaming in the morning sun.

Carter had said and done nothing while Mark, Toz and Lenny abused Emma the evening before. She hadn't seemed to object: in fact she had participated in all their activities, so he supposed she must have liked it. It was obviously not the first time, and yet she'd come back for more. The lads had their fill of her, and once they'd finished Mark kicked her out of the room. She asked to stay a little longer but Mark told her to leave, so she left: no escort, just out the door! The three lads had joked a bit about what they'd done, how tight she was, and how they had got her to do things. Then they slept for a few hours before going out. Carter had stayed on his bed, sleeping on and off until they left.

Once they were out of the way, he got up and went to Jonah's room, where the door was now open. When he told him what had happened, and about the girl, Jonah just smiled. 'That's Toz! Bit of a nasty bastard. He was never going to like you. Him and Mickey were close, and he was a bit miffed when Mickey transferred to become a Tech. Don't worry about Emma, she's a nympho. Half the barracks has been through her, and she loves it. Weird if you ask me, but the boys like her, and if they can't pull a girl, it's her they always have. A few beers and fags and she'll do anything they want. And don't worry about Toz messing you about either; I'll have a word with him.'

The squad was called to attention by a stocky sergeant with an aggressive growl, who was joined a couple of seconds later by a tall, wiry young man of about twenty. The sergeant saluted the officer and told him the troop was ready for inspection. "Ok Sergeant", he responded, "Carry on!" The sergeant then started a roll call, to which each of the men responded with "Present!" or "Here!" and as the names were being called, Carter's mind drifted back to first thing that morning.

It had started at around six when the first alarm squawked, followed by a groan and slamming of hand to silence the noise. This was followed by another alarm a few seconds later, which this time was left to shrill. Bodies started to moan, and Carter could see Lenny's hand appear from beneath his duvet, searching for and then locating his cigarettes. There was the click of a lighter, a flicker of light, and then the sound of an intake of breath. Carter swung his legs out of bed and got up. Putting on his dressing gown, he grabbed wash kit and towel from his locker and headed for the wash rooms.

As he had memorably discovered soon after he first arrived, these consisted of two white tiled areas. In one was a row of open showers with six shower nozzles protruding from the wall, chrome push buttons half-way down and temperature dials just above. The other sported a row of urinals at the far end below a frost-ed window, and six cubicled toilets opposite a row of sinks and mirrors. The shower room already had three occupants, their towels and dressing gowns hanging from hooks on the opposite wall. Carter noticed that all three looked lean and muscled. No one really paid much attention to him as he got under the shower, the initial burst of cold making his muscles contract in shock. Then he let the now warming water hit the top of his head, comforting his face as it poured over him. Gradually acclimatising to his present surroundings, he seemed to be losing the need or want for luxury, yet only a year ago he would have never dreamed of living in these conditions. This wash block reminded him of the changing rooms of his school gym, but though old and well used like them, they were not dirty. Nothing in the Army was dirty.

As he was washing he saw Toz come in, his eyes lin-gering on Carter as he walked past to hang up his kit. What was it with that guy! Next Mark hung his towels up and climbed under the shower at the end of the row near the window. Lastly came Jonah, greeting Carter as he took the shower next to him. Carter washed his body and hair, and then went to the sinks to have a shave and clean his teeth.

Now he was recalled to the present by the voice of the sergeant. "We have three new Nigs joining us today: Carter, Smith and Peterson, fall out and come up the front!" Carter did a right turn and then marched to the front of the squad, where he was joined by two others he had not seen on the plane, or on the bus to the barracks. "OK, what I want you three to do is introduce yourselves to the troop. Name, number, trade, where you're from in the UK, and then something interesting about yourself. Peterson, you start!"

Peterson was a skinny eighteen year old with a crew cut, and his eyes looked a bit far apart. "I'm Jack Peterson, 24828942, from Cromer in Norfolk", explained the eyes, and Carter smiled to himself. "I am a radio relay operator. Something interesting about myself: I tried out for the Junior Canaries before I joined up"

"A footballer, good! Come and see me later, and you can have a try out for the regimental team. Smith, now for you!"

Smith spoke up. Shorter than Peterson, but you could see he was built well, or was bulking up. For an eighteen year old he was pretty muscly. "I'm Peter Smith, 'Smudge' as everyone calls me, 24828854. I am a power man, and I'm from Hull. Something interesting.... Er, I once won a competition to meet Tom Baker from Doctor Who" This generated some mutters and giggles, and the odd "Geek!" from the men.

"Now you, Carter!"

"Morning….."

"Toff!" Carter heard Toz's voice somewhere in the squad.

"My name is Chris Carter, 2482867. I am a technician…."

"Wanker!" Toz's voice again, and some chuckles.

"I am from Debden in Essex."

"Southern pansy!"

"Something Interesting……" Carter was now desperately trying to think of something to say about himself - something witty, something clever, but there was nothing……what could he say! "I once came second in an annual school writing competition for Essex."

"Tosser!" Toz again, with a number of sniggers and groans from the rest of the squad.

The sergeant turned to the three of them. "Ok you three, go in and parade outside the troop office! Mr Harrington will speak to each of you in turn after the parade." Turning smartly, they marched back towards the troop offices and stood outside, waiting in awkward silence.

Smudge and Peterson were seen first, and then as Peterson left the office Carter's name was called. He marched into a room with two desks at one end, positioned in front of high sash windows. The officer Harrington sat at one, with the behind the other. On reaching the officer's desk Carter came to a halt, slamming his left leg into the ground, and then saluted to Army regulation standards.

"At ease, Carter. My name is Lieutenant Harrington and I am your Troop Commander. This is Panther Troop, and you are part of 1 Squadron Radio Relay Squadron. We are part of 4th Armoured Division and Signal Squadron, the forward combat division separating Western Europe from the Communist East. We tend to be on exercise nine months of the year. Have you got a girlfriend back in the UK?"

"Yes, Sir!"

"Expect it to last another couple of months max before she ends up sleeping with your best mate back home. If she's a healthy young girl she won't be waiting around for you to rock up six weeks of the year. If I were you, I'd forget her now and find your kicks over here."

Harrington watched Carter's reaction. He could normally tell if he had a 'Dear John' case on his hands. Too many of the young lads went off the rails, or tried to get back to the UK once they received the inevitable letter from the girl friend saying she still loved them but couldn't live without them, so was now seeing someone else.

"All I expect from you is to be a good soldier. Keep fit, keep clean, keep smart, and be good at your job. I have a report here that tells me you were top of your class in training and are potential foreman material. That was training, this is now: before anything else, you need to prove you're a good soldier." There was a pause as the officer again seemed to be studying him. "Over the next few weeks we will settle you in, and you also have some signatures to get down on your joining instructions," Harrington pushed some paperwork across his desk. "You have a BFT and CFT to do, and weapons training. The Technicians are based in the cellar where your workshop is, and where you need to report to Staff Sergeant Gant. This is Sergeant Bickerstaff, standing in for Staff Sergeant Green who is away on a training course at the moment. The paperwork requiring signatures introduces you to the personalities you need to know around the barracks. Make sure it's all signed by the end of the week. I have signed my part; you need Bickerstaff's signature too, and then off you go!"

"Thank you, Sir!" Carter saluted and turned to

Sergeant Bickerstaff, a balding man in his early thirties; fit looking, with a wiry frame and a weathered face. "Could you sign my joining instructions, Sergeant?"

"If you say 'please'." Bickerstaff glared at Carter.

"Please!"

"Please what?" Bickerstaff growled.

"Could you sign my joining instructions, please, Sergeant?"

"*IF* you march over here, stand to attention and hand me the paperwork correctly, Corporal! I am not your fucking mate!"

For a second Carter just looked at the Sergeant. What was it with this place! Everyone seemed to be just so angry with him. Then he marched up to Bickerstaff's desk, halted three steps away did a right turn and handed over the paperwork. "Could you sign my joining instructions, please, Sergeant?"

"Of course, Corporal!" smiled Bickerstaff, signing in Green's name. "Now off you go and see Staff Sergeant Gant."

***

The next two weeks flew by. Carter spent the first few days working his way round the barracks gathering signatures for his forms. Some were easier to get than others, but one thing that collecting them did show him was that the army was made up of an eclectic mix of characters. As well as the full-on army types you would expect, there were others who seemed not to want to be there but had somehow ended up in uniform. This surprised Carter, considering you had to go through a selection process before you even started Basics. There were fit lads, lazy lads, and post-injury lads. Some were friendly, others weren't, and some were just odd. It certainly wasn't what he had expected.

Part of the two weeks was completing his Basic Soldiering Tests, Combat Fitness Test and Basic Fitness Test (BFT). He passed the first two with ease and the BFT in 7minutes 40 Seconds, which was not a bad time for one and half miles in boots. Carter also showed a good eye on the range, and scored highly with SLR, SMG and the Browning nine millimetre pistol.

Something else he discovered during those initial two weeks was that he was going to hate his job. The technical workshop was in the basement of the living accommodation. Staff Sergeant Gant who was in charge of the technicians of his squadron, was nearing the end of his twenty-two year service and had lost all interest in the Army. At the age of thirty-eight Gant had a pension in the offing, and nothing on his mind but marking time. He had a beer belly on him and did the minimum required to get by. He was always accompanied by two Sergeant Technicians, the three of them spending most of the day in his basement office smoking and playing the card game Hearts.

When he first met Carter he looked him up and down, signed his form, and asked him to find Sergeant Lemington, who swiftly showed him where the soldering iron, solder, cables and earth lugs were. "Make up 20 earth cables, all the length of 5 metres. If you don't rush it, should take you all week." The technical troop of a squadron ensured that all the equipment worked when it was on exercise. As the technicians in this squadron did not have any of the bench testing equipment, anything seriously faulty was sent to the TM (Technical Maintenance) Troop, so Carter's life was spent fixing damaged cables, or connecting earth lugs onto them. Nothing he needed to use a brain for.

Carter felt completely trapped. Having signed up in the Recruiting Office for nine years, he was now stuck in this regiment with nothing better to do than fix cables on a daily basis. To make bad worse, he shared a room with three lads that went out of their way not to like him: in the last two weeks this had not abated at all. What was he going to do?

Chapter 6

Carter walked onto the square with his Bergen on his back, rifle under his arm and wearing his webbing. It was 04:00hrs and the air was crisp. There were eight rows of vehicles on the square, Bedford four- tonners in four of them, with 432 tracked armoured vehicles in the others. The vehicles had been lined up the evening before ready for the start of the exercise at 04:30hrs. There was already plenty of activity air going on - kit being loaded into the back of vehicles and engines being fired up. Carter found his vehicle, a Bedford four tonner with a big box on the back; this was the switch vehicle. Though it sat on the back of a four tonne Bedford, the lorry itself weighed more than eight tonnes. Carter was to be the driver during the exercise, having got his HGV licence as part of his training.

Tam was already on board, smoking a cigarette in the passenger seat. He was a skinny runt of a man from Aberdeen in Scotland, openly admitting that he had joined the Army to get out of the drugs scene that was taking over his estate. He had been recruited as a boy soldier, had gone to Harrogate, and was now working his way up the ranks as an operator. He was pleasant enough, but did like his drinking and enjoyed a bit of a fight too. His long-suffering wife, another Aberdonian, just put up with him. After all, she had a better life here in Germany than in Scotland, and Tam was a nice guy when he was not off the rails.

"Hi Carter!" Tam smiled. " Ready for another six weeks in this blue coffin?"

Carter smiled in return as he walked to the back of the wagon, opened up the door and slung his Bergen in the back before going round to the passenger door. After chucking his rifle and webbing behind the driver's seat, he climbed up into the cab and the wagon was ready to go. Now they just had to sit there waiting for the time for the exercise to start. The German law was that HGVs were not allowed on the motorways on a Sunday, so back roads had to be used to get to the exercise location; it was sixty kilometres away, which in this vehicle meant about a two hour drive.

Tam said nothing, Carter said nothing. At last at 04:30hrs the first of the convoys fired up their engines and pulled off the square. Carter's lorry was the fourth in his convoy, and as soon as he saw the brake lights illuminate on the vehicle in front of his he fired the Bedford into life. Then they pulled off the square and made their way out of the barracks, turning left and heading out of town.

As soon as the four-tonner got to the hills it began struggling with its weight, and Carter kept having to go up and down the gear box between third and fourth gear. Clutch in, clutch out continuously, the vehicle could barely manage 30 mph. Tam lit yet another cigarette, Carter's throat already feeling rough from the many he'd already smoked. He kept his window fully open to minimise the effect of the smoke in the cab, but stoically said nothing!

Three hours later the convoy pulled up along the road outside a farm yard. This was a regular location used by the troop, and the farmer was well paid by the Military for the use of his barns and yards. Sergeant Bickerstaff came along the line of vehicles, checking them off. The one in front of Carter began to move and before long he was manoeuvring his own lorry into a barn, where the vehicles were being parked up bumper to bumper. This had been done so many times before that it was second pat for the sergeant to guide them in.

Once the vehicles were installed and powered up, and the generators set rumbling, the barn became a hive of activity. Carter's job was to go and set up the SHF radio link from the switch vehicle to the radio relay vehicle up in the hills. He grabbed the antenna and the SHF radio from the trailer, and the 'power man' in charge of the generators helped him carry over the 500Kw generator used to power it.

Using his compass, he took the bearing for the radio relay vehicle he had identified on his map, and then located a spot at the corner of the yard to place the antenna for the SHF radio. He unpacked the antenna, assembled it and raised it to its full height before connecting the radio. Next he set all the frequencies on the radio set and powered it up. The radio relay wagon would have been in location and set up hours before. Using his signal power monitor to locate the signal from the wagon, he began to swing the SHF antenna in 180 degree swings, looking for a twitch in the monitor's needle. When he saw the needle spike on the monitor he stopped the antenna at that location, and then got the maximum strength for the signal with minimal moves of the antenna: it was like getting a good signal for a TV antenna at home. Once it was at its strongest, he started lowering the antenna to its minimum height with the good signal. In time of war, a signal node would need to be as camouflaged as possible. As soon as he was happy that he had the best signal and the maximum low height for the antenna, the SHF radio kit was covered up with a black plastic bag to waterproof it. When it came out of the factory the SHF radio equipment was vacuum sealed, but once opened in MT Troop to fix a fault, it could not be sealed properly again. They always went faulty because of water ingress. The generator was checked for fuel, and there was a spare Gerry can provided that would need to be swopped over in about four hours.

Carter now made his way back to the switch vehicle, where Tam was programming in the last of the links to other signal nodes. The vehicle communicated with the rest of the network through the SHF link that Carter had just set up. The Royal Signals had set up for the battle field a communications system called Ptarmigan - a military version of a mobile phone network. Using his radio, any infantry soldier could now communicate from the front line with anyone, anywhere who also had a network connection. On major exercises you could even communicate with Whitehall, as the network was connected to the public phone system.

Once all switch vehicles were linked to the surrounding nodes, Tam sat back in his chair. "That's it for the next six weeks; we now sit here in this blue coffin doing f'all." The 'blue coffin' was the name given to the switch vehicle, the central computer system for their node: the hub computer, or brains of the node. It was a walk-in machine decked out in blue. The operators sat in front of a small computer screen at the end of the vehicle, which detailed the status of the communication links with other nodes, and the rest of the vehicle was made up of computer components. A modern day laptop would be more than powerful enough to cope with what this whole vehicle processed.

The exercise was to lay down communications for the battle groups while they played war games. The Royal Signals were white troops, neutral, so not part of the battle. They just maintained communications until an 'End-ex' signal was relayed to denote the end of the exercise, and then everyone packed up and went back to barracks.

"You might as well go and see if the cook has set up, Carter, and fetch me a sausage sandwich," Tam said, "and find the rest of the guys and get them back here, so I can draw up a roster"

He duly made his way out of the switch vehicle and into the barn, which now housed four four-tonner lorries and two Land Rovers. As well as the Switch, there were the Technical Maintenance Wagon, the Command Wagon, which was backed up to the Switch, and the power man's vehicle. The Land Rovers were the Officers' and the recce Land Rover, used to visit radio relay sites.

Carter went on out into the court yard, which was made up of the barn where the wagons were parked, a shed which housed a number of cows and another long brick building by the front gate. This had been utilised as the Admin Area and Sleeping Quarters. There was a normal sized entrance built into the hefty barn doors, and ongoing in he was surprised to see that a large canvas tent had been erected. A Four-Tonner was parked in the barn, and there were benches and tables set up in the tent. This area was now the cookhouse and chill- out area, with the cook in the last stages of setting up his field kitchen next to the lorry.

The barn smelt of animals and hay: there was actually a donkey in a stall at the far end by the cook's wagon! Pete, the power man that had helped him set up the SHF radio, was working on setting up a TV screen with a VHS video attached. It was one of those large, back-lit screens powered by three coloured bulbs. When the screen came alive the picture showed a young girl stepping out of her dress, and Carter smiled. What was with it with all these blokes! They were obsessed with pornography. As he made his way over to the cook, he noticed that the girl who had just undressed was now on her knees in front of two black men in builders' gear. The cook was perspiring from the heat of the burners he had fired up, and which were now heating two large containers of water. "Hi there! I'm Carter. Don't think we've met," Carter smiled.

"Micky!" the sweating cook smiled back. "If you're after food for Tam, give me another hour. I'm just getting the brews on." And he looked over Carter's shoulder to see what the girl on the screen was getting up to. "Ok, I'll tell him, and be back in hour." The girl on the TV was now sucking the two black men's cocks one after the other, and Pete the Powerman was sitting in front of the screen smoking a cigarette.

Carter moved further on into the shed, where more tents were being set up for sleeping accommodation. Then he thought twice about showing his face, and reversed his steps. He didn't want to get roped into a work detail; he would rather be back at the switch doing nothing than helping erect tents. As he left the Mess area, Girl on the Screen was being mounted by both black men and Pete was on his second cigarette.

Back at the switch wagon, Tam had a beer in his hand and was smoking a cigarette. "Aren't these dry exercises?" Carter asked.

"They are," came the reply, "but if you don't take this piss, no-one really cares. Everyone has a few. You should spend time with the radio relay wagons! They're up there on their own with even less to do than we have. At least our day's broken up by meals cooked by someone else, and the guard rota. You want a beer, they're behind the grille of the air con unit. Keeps them cool!"

Carter undid the screws of the grille with his fingers, took a bottle of Herforder beer, and sat down next to Tam, who passed him a church key.

"There's fuck all for us to do now for six weeks, except we get a few shower breaks in the local pool and one trip back to barracks for an overnight break. It's not like a Signals group exercise, where you're moving the whole time, every 12 hours, move, set up Comms, move again. Just sit and chill - read a book. All we need to do is make sure those genies keep the SHF link up. Not a bad job if you ask me!"

"Not what they sell you in the Careers Office."

"Yeah! They sell being in the fucking jungle with your weapons as an adventure. Fuck that, I was in Belize when I was with 30 Sigs and got bitten by a fuck-off snake; had to be flown to Miami for a anti-venom shot. I'd rather be doing this. Eat, drink, smoke, read and watch porn, and get paid for it!"

"But there's got to be more to life than this!"

"If you think so, why did you join up, you Muppet!" Tam smiled. "You take first stint in the coffin, and I'll go and find the guys and see what filth they've brought out for entertainment."

Carter sat back in his chair with his beer and stared at the green computer screen, while all around him the vehicle system hummed its dreary rhythms.

***

By the time two weeks had passed, Carter was well into his routine. The switch vehicle was manned on a twenty-four hour shift pattern, Tam having set it for an 8am until 8pm, and then 8pm until 8am rota. Carter had been put on the night pattern with Jenkins, a systems operator like Tam, but a private. He had been in the army for four years and was just waiting to be promoted to lance corporal. A quiet lad, he didn't have a lot to say, but didn't think much of Carter just because he was a technician. Like any good soldier, Jenkins never questioned what he was told to do, and if he was told not to like Carter, then he would *not* like Carter - until someone told him different. Jenkins read books, smoked cigarettes, drank some beer and did not really talk. Carter found the best part of the shift was replenishing the generator for the SHF radio; he volunteered to do that each time, so he could get some fresh air and enjoy the night sky away from the hum of the switch vehicle.

Nothing had happened in those two weeks; nothing had changed as they sat in the wagon all night and every night. He had done guard duties for two hour stints at the entrance to the farmyard, but again nothing much happened. The occasional vehicle passed by, but at that time of night nobody was really about. He went to his meals, which were almost invariably accompanied by the inevitable porn. Occasionally a film was put on, but they only seemed to have two: 'The Good the Bad and the Ugly' and 'The Blues Brothers'. The lads knew the words to these films off by heart and sometimes watched them with the sound off, miming the words to each other around the table. Then the porn was back on. How many times could they enjoy seeing a young blonde girl be gang- banged by a group of black men? Seeing that most of the lads here were inherently racist, why would they enjoy watching this over and over again!

Carter had nearly finished a book by Sven Hassel, and was enjoying reading about Sven's time on the Russian Front. It was nothing like his life in the blue coffin, which was so different from what he had expected. He looked at the clock on the side of the wagon: it was two am, and his two hour guard duty didn't start until three. He had filled the generator an hour ago, so there was nothing left to do, but put the kettle on for another coffee.

A couple of days later he was in the makeshift cook house, trying to zone out the porn while having his lunch of stew, when Sergeant Bickerstaff asked if he would like to join him on a drive around the radio relay sites, to drop off some mail and supplies. Of course he jumped at the opportunity, and an hour later found himself driving the long wheel based Land Rover with Sergeant Bickerstaff navigating, map laid out on his lap.

"So, how you enjoying the Army, Carter?" Bickerstaff asked. "You must have been with us a couple of months now."

"It's ok", Carter lied. "Just getting used to being here and getting to know the lads."

"Funny lot, some of the lads. I was glad to get married and out the block. Never suited me, living in the block. Some of the lads are like animals."

Carter just grunted. "Yep!"

"Don't worry about it. You've got your T2 exam to take in a few months, and then you'll be a full screw and should get your own room. You're sharing with Toz and his crew now, aren't you, and they're a bit on the rough side. Staff Sergeant Green wanted you in with them. I said it wouldn't be a good idea, but he was mates with Micky and they kept in touch when he was on his tech course. You and Micky didn't get on did you?"

Carter shook his head.

"Don't worry about Staff Green; you should be alright with him. You're a soldier- shoot well, one of the fittest in the troop. He'll be talking you into applying for 264 or 216 before long."

Carter nodded: he was dreading the appearance of Staff Green. He had been told that he couldn't stand technicians, and even his own seniors in the basement did not talk kindly of the man.

"Take a left up here, and then there's a dirt track about 200 metres on the right. That's the track to our first site."

It took them another twenty minutes to reach the radio relay wagon parked in a clearing in the wood, its antenna at full height. The noise of the generator exhaust filled the air in that quiet, leafy place. One of the operators lay on top of the vehicle, reading a book; the other was listening to music in the back of the wagon. Sergeant Bickerstaff said hi, and introduced Carter. He had a chat for a bit, dropped off some mail and handed over a crate of beer. There were some smiles and waves, and then it was off to find the next location.

The second wagon was Toz's, Lenny and Mark with him. They were all at the back of the wagon, sitting on foldaway chairs enjoying the sun. As soon as they had been given their mail and beer Toz broke open the beers and offered one to Sergeant Bickerstaff, who said, "Why not!" The sergeant sat on the back steps of the radio wagon and Carter sat on the ground.

"How's it been, Toz?" Bickerstaff asked.

"Good, Sarge!" Toz grinned. "Love these static exercises. Six weeks here is like a holiday. We've got to know some of the locals, and have a BBQ most evenings. The local girls seem to know when we're here, and round they come like moths to a lamp!"

"I don't want any trouble like there was a few months ago, Toz", Bickerstaff stated.

"You know that wasn't my fault. What am I supposed to do when someone attacks me?" Toz moaned.

"Don't shag their fucking wife!"

"She was up here walking the dog every day, and just got more and more friendly. Then one day her husband followed her – I think the dog walks were getting a bit long." Toz smiled.

"Just be a bit more discreet. You don't want your promotion delayed again."

"What can I do, if it's offered on a plate? I *have* to take it!"

"Ok Toz, and I *have* warned you." Bickerstaff got up. "You just be careful!"

After getting back into the Land Rover Sergeant Bickerstaff said, "I don't know how that little shit does it. He and his little gang are always at it. That husband that followed his wife: it wasn't just Toz; it was Toz and the rest of his crew with her."

"I can imagine. They're always at it as a group. I don't think I've ever seen Toz with a girl unless his cronies are with him."

"Odd little fucker! Beat the husband up a bit when he walked in on them all with his wife, so he called the local police, who arrested the lot of them for assault." Bickerstaff smiled. "Staff Green and the CO went ballistic – but each to their own."

"Try living with them!"

They visited a further three wagons, one of them Jonah's. He was happy to see Carter, and they all sat around for a bit while Jonah made bacon sarnies and they sat washing them down with a beer. Carter relaxed, enjoying the sun and listening to the sounds of the woods, while Jonah chatted about nothing in particular.

Carter just could not get out of his mind how brain numbingly boring life in the Army was. He was trying his hardest to get his mind set into it, four weeks into the exercise and it was still just routine boredom. He had even been reduced to re-reading some of the books that were lying about. The best part of the exercise had been when he was allowed back to barracks for a night off. He'd been on the same relief detail as Jonah, and they had arranged to go out for the night when they sat together in the back of the Landrover on the way back to barracks.

Once there, he had loaded two washing machines with his dirty clothes, stripped off and stood under the shower for half an hour, desperate to clear away the smell and grime of living in the same clothes week after week.

Soap and more soap; shampoo in the hair – more! Soaping the skin; smelling the perfume of the soap. Once out of the shower, Carter shaved and washed his face again. He looked into his eyes. The shine was going from his face, or was it fatigue? He needed to get out, interact, and have some excitement.

Jonah knocked on his door around eight. "Come on then, let's go and find us some fun!" They left the barracks and headed down to the town on foot. Jonah had said, "I know this quiet little pub, and then we'll go on to the Go-Park and find some nice talent." Carter just followed.

As soon as Jonah entered the pub, the German barman, who was also the owner, welcomed him with a smile and by name. "This is my good friend Carter!" Jonah slapped Carter on the back. "And this is Klaus.

He is the fine patron of this bar! Line up three beers each on the counter please, my good man!"

Klaus and Jonah spoke in German to each other, Carter picking up a little of what they said. Klaus was moaning about some sort of trouble that had happened down town between a bunch of British squaddies and a few of the locals. Jonah defended both parties by reckoning it was probably all high spirits, and they were all as bad as each other. Some of the local lads enjoyed squaddie bashing, and would seek out one soldier on his own and beat him. Klaus declared he wished all British soldiers were like Jonah. All three raised a beer to that, with some of the locals in the bar joining in, then after about an hour and half and a few more beers, Jonah and Carter made their way into the town.

"We need to find two girls to walk us into the club," Jonah stated. "Klaus said none of the local clubs are allowing British soldiers in at the moment. The Tankies from 16/5th Lancers were in town on the Saturday before the exercise and smashed the place up a bit. The clubs were pissed off, and the locals aren't too happy either. We need to pay the entry for a couple of girls, buy them a drink, and then send them on their merry way. They just have to pretend to be our girlfriends when we go in."

Jonah and Carter stood at the side of the road not far from the club, and when some girls came by Jonah approached them, speaking in German. Most waved him away, with 'Nein, nein! English!" but eventually he managed to keep a couple of young girls talking. One of them, a young blonde, looked quite provocatively at Carter, who smiled back, and they agreed to escort them into the club in return for the entry fee and a drink. The blonde was about nineteen; she had long hair, a fresh face and was dressed in a smart casual dress that showed her figure off - but not "in your face".

Once inside, she sidled up to Carter, "Name?"

"Chris Carter. And you?"

"Lemska."? She smiled back, taking Carters hand.

"Ok Lemska, nice to meet you!" Carter smiled back.

When they arrived at the club the doormen were not letting Jonah and Carter in. "No English!" one of them grunted. The two girls dived into action, telling them that they were with the boys. Lemska began arguing with one of the doormen; then she grabbed Carter, pulled him close and started kissing him. He kissed her back, and she seemed to respond to him, which apparently satisfied the doorman, who said 'Ja, ja! Eintreten!" and the two girls led the way to the ticket booth. Jonah paid for four entries and then for the cloak room. The group then made their way into the thumping club, where there were no other British lads about because of the curfew. Jonah headed for the bar, where he bought four drinks; Carter sat on a bar stool and Lemska positioned herself between his legs. "You are a pretty man, Chris!" She ran her hand down his cheek. "You like to dance? You want to dance with me?" Jonah smiled behind Lemska and raised his glass. Ingrid Green stood at the edge of the dance floor with her friend Suzie. Her husband, Staff Green, was due back tomorrow and she knew this would be her last night out for a while. Watching Carter with the young girl, she knew how she wanted to spend her last night of freedom.

Carter needed a drink. Lemska had made him stay put, dancing around him, moving up close to him, generally enjoying herself. Her enjoyment was infectious. He liked the look of Lemska: liked the way she moved; liked her smile; liked the way she seemed to be enjoying herself. By now, the heat and smoke were drying his throat, and he moved in towards her and asked if she would like a drink. Lemska smiled, touched his cheek and nodded, so he led her bar, where they found Jonah, now on his own, drinking beer out of bottle.

Jonah bought a round of drinks, and then Lemska looked at her watch and told Carter she needed to leave in about half an hour. It was getting late and she wanted to be home before midnight. Carter and Lemska started talking, while Jonah sat on a bar stool just seeming to enjoy the music and the atmosphere of the club. After a quarter of an hour or so, Lemska passed Carter a bar napkin with her number written on it. "Can you call me tomorrow? I would like to get to know you a bit better, Chris," she smiled. Then she kissed him on the cheek, and left to find her friend before going home.

"Bit of a result, my man!" Jonah smiled" Quite a hot looking one!" Carter smiled back. He hadn't really talked much to Lemska, just found out she was nineteen and lived with her parents about eight miles from Herford. He decided he would give her a call tomorrow.

As Carter and Jonah stood at the bar, not talking to each other, just listening to the music, two women walked over. One was blonde, rather drunk and heavily made up, and with a top and skirt that left little to the imagination. The other, who was dark haired and rather elegant in comparison, said hello to Jonah.

"Hello Ingrid! Hi Suzie! What are you two doing out tonight?"

"Alan's back tomorrow," said the one he'd called Ingrid, "I thought I'd have one last night out before he gets home." She smiled. "Before it all gets back to normal! Are you going to introduce me to your friend?"

"Ah!" Jonah looked at her for a moment before introducing Carter. "This is Carter. New boy, not been here five minutes." He turned to Carter. "Ingrid and Suzie! Ingrid is the better half of Al Green, better known as Staff Sergeant Green. You haven't met yet - been on his drill course. And this is Suzie. She's married to one of the Tankies from the 16/5th." Ingrid positioned herself closer to Carter; Suzie looked Jonah up and down, placed a finger on her lips, pointed at him, and then touched his chest. He smiled, winked at Carter, and asked the two women if they would care for a drink. After a few minutes of chat, Suzie asked if they would like to join them in the snug. Jonah agreed and Carter followed. He had never been in a place like this, and he was amazed. The club was enormous; it had five dance floors, a number of different themed bars, and an area where you could buy such food as pizzas, ice cream, and hot dogs.

Suzie led the way into a room full of comfortable sofas and chairs. The red, yellow and orange lights were dimmed, and the music in the background was soft and light. They managed to find an empty sofa, separated from another by a low table. Opposite them were three men and a young girl, talking quietly amongst themselves. As soon as Jonah sat down, Suzie dropped beside him, leaving Carter to sit next to Ingrid. Suzie snuggled right up to Jonah, but Carter still felt uncomfortable in such close proximity to this married woman. Jonah didn't seem to have any issues, though. Suzie was a married woman but from one of the other regiments, so was fair game. Ingrid, on the other hand, was his Staff Sergeant's wife. What was he supposed to do? What were they doing even entertaining these girls? Why not just stay at the bar, have a drink, have a chat and then go and find some local talent.

"So how are you enjoying 4 Div Carter?" Ingrid asked.

"Do you want the truth, or the model answer! You're the wife of Staff Green, aren't you?"

"No need to be touchy! What's your first name?" Ingrid smiled and gently touched Carter's leg.

"Chris."

"Well, that's better than 'Carter! Calm yourself down, Chris. The world you've just joined isn't the same as the world you've just left. The rules, and the way things are done here are a lot different. So let me ask you again. How are you enjoying 4 Div?"

"To tell you the truth, it's not what I expected. It's a lot easier physically, and a lot more boring than I imagined. I had it in my head it was going to be a Boys' Own adventure, and here I am sitting in the back of a blue coffin for twelve hours a day in a farm shed."

Ingrid smiled. "But it *is* still a job, and it *does* have its fringe benefits," and she nodded over to where Jonah was sitting. By now he was all over Suzie, looking like he was eating her as he kissed her, and with his hand up her skirt. The locals on the other sofa seemed oblivious, just carrying on with their own quiet conversation.

"Well, it's odd, and I've never known anything like it. I remember going out in Catterick to the night club just outside the barracks. Buses turned up full of girls from towns all around. It's not like it was at home before I joined."

Ingrid smiled. "It's like I said, the rules are different now, and the way of life is different. The girls who came on those buses, they'd do anything if they thought it would bag a soldier. It'd get them out of the council estates; away from their families and mundane jobs. For some it's the only escape from the lives their parents have been stuck in for years"

"Yeah, I understand that, but look at Suzie with Jonah. She's married, and that's not right!"

"She's twenty-one, got married at eighteen. Her husband's a knob and treats her like shit. She knows he'll be on exercise nine months of the year, so when he's away Suzie just likes to have a bit of fun, and a bit of warmth."

"It is still not right. What would her husband say?"

"He'd try and kill Jonah and give Suzie a good kicking. She's already been beaten a few times, but it is not all it seems either. Her husband's part of a group on the patch who have parties where they swop wives about. So who's right and who's wrong? He is happy enough to whore her out at a party."

"Still, this is all a bit fucked up, and if they had told me what it would be like when I first walked in that recruiting office, I'd have run a mile"

"So why did you join?"

"Mum and dad split up. My dad earned too much money for me to get a grant to go to Uni, and he said he wouldn't pay for me to be a ponce for three years. He told me if I wanted a career, join the Army, get a trade and become a man. The same as he did."

"What was he in?"

"He was in National Service, Royal Engineers. He's an engineer now, building motorways and bridges."

"So you're a clever one; should be at Uni and all that. This definitely isn't the place to be if you're clever. It'll suck the life out of you."

Jonah suddenly came up for air. "You getting the round in?"

"Will do!"

"I'll help you get the drinks," said Ingrid, standing up with him. "Save our seats!" she shouted over to Jonah, who smiled back with his arm around Susie's shoulders.

Ingrid walked towards the bar, Carter admiring her athletic shape from behind. He still felt uncomfortable being seen with her: she was not only a married woman, but married to his Staff Sergeant. She must have been about six years older than him too. When he ordered the drinks at the bar, he couldn't help but look Ingrid up and down. She had dark shoulder length hair, a slim waist and small breasts that were tight against her silk top. Her skin was clear and white.

"So where are you from?" Carter asked.

"Norway. I met Al when he was on a training course there."

"That's a long way to come!"

"Like the girls that came to Catterick on the buses! There was nothing for me in Norway, and it was my way out."

"Have you got kids?"

"One little boy, Matthew. He's five and half now."

"That's a nice name."

"Well, don't let's talk about that now. What do you like to do for fun, Chris?"

"I like to read, walk for hours in the countryside, swim, ski, run, shoot! That's why I thought it would be great to join the Army."

"You *can* do all those things, but not that often. There is the two week ski holiday everyone goes on each year; then there is summer camp for two weeks. Range days, but the rest of the time you're in your wagons."

"What do you like to do?"

"When I am not being a mother and a wife, I like to have fun!" Ingrid winked and smiled.

Carter blushed, and Ingrid lightly touched his arm.

"Don't worry! You're an odd one, though. None of the guys I know hold back when it's offered on a plate."

When they got back to the sofa the group of locals had gone and Jonah was being a bit more adventurous with his hands.

"See what I mean!" smiled Ingrid.

Carter could hardly believe this: in effect, Ingrid was asking him why he wasn't trying it on. Was it just him? Was there something wrong with him? Jonah seemed to have no qualms about what he was up to.

When they sat down Ingrid moved closer to him, resting her hand on Carter's thigh. He felt very uncomfortable, but let it stay. He slowly sipped his beer, watching as Jonah's hand worked under Suzie's skirt. Suzie was sucking Jonah's earlobe. Carter wondered what to do next; he thought back to Lemska, and then glanced sidelong at Ingrid.

Jonah suddenly announced they were leaving. Carter looked at his watch: it was two in the morning. Jonah led the way holding on to Suzie, and Ingrid took hold of Carter's hand. As they were going out Carter happened to catch the eye of the doorman who'd let them in. He shook his head and pointed to his eyes, and then at Carter. This seemed strange: why would the doorman make such an effort to let Carter know that he'd clocked him?

Once outside, Jonah asked the girls how they had arrived. Ingrid told him by taxi, so Jonah said they would walk them to the taxi rank. This meant cutting through the underpass Carter had been in the first time he went to the club, and he felt uncomfortable now he guessed what Jonah was up to. His heart rate increased as they walked down the steps to the entrance; it didn't seem right to be holding the hand of this married woman. Once in the underpass, Jonah and Suzie stopped, as Carter knew they would. Jonah had his hands on Suzie's shoulders, pushing her down, and Carter heard the sound of his zip being undone. Ingrid was smiling at him now, and taking Carter's head in her hands she pulled him forward. Opening her own mouth just slightly and moving her tongue into his mouth, she kissed him. Carter submitted, letting his hands go around her waist.

Ingrid moved her body up closer, until Carter felt her

breasts against his chest. She moved his arms from her waist, guiding them upwards, and at this point Carter gave in. He slid his hands under her top, pushed her light bra up and nipped her nipples with his finger and thumb. Ingrid gave out a sigh and pushed her hand down to his cock, rubbing it through his trousers before unzipping them and holding it in her hand. By now he was hard, and almost before he realised what was happening, he felt her wet opening on the tip. He resisted slightly, but Ingrid moved herself onto him, one leg up around his side, and Carter was in her. In his head he didn't want to do this, but the feeling of Ingrid on his cock took over. He found himself thrusting in and out of her, and before long he came. He pushed hard and Ingrid moaned; he felt her shudder on him, and as he pulled out he had to hold her close because her legs were weak.

"Now, that wasn't too bad, was it!" Ingrid whispered in his ear. He looked over to Jonah, who was still thrusting in out of Suzie's mouth. Carter could not say anything.

Jonah suddenly came. When he was finished Suzie stood up, and then asked 'where to next?' Ingrid said she was going home, and Carter agreed. He just wanted to get back to the barracks. Jonah asked Suzie if she wanted to go back there with him, and she readily agreed.

When they got to the taxi rank, Carter kissed Ingrid good bye, and he, Suzie and Jonah got into another cab and headed back to the barracks. Jonah and Suzie were on the back seat, and Jonah looked like he was being naughty just for the sake of it. He had Suzie's top lifted up so the taxi driver could get a full view of her ample breasts. The driver, a guy in his fifties, smiled at Carter, who just shrugged, and then adjusted his mirror for a better view of the scene in the back seat.

When they got back to the barracks, Carter was glad to see his bed, and for once the room was his own for the night. He slept heavily, but his dreams were not comfortable. He thought he was stuck in a room full of people, his arms tied as they pointed and laughed at him.

Chapter 7

The dawn air was crisp, the sun just breaking above the horizon in the first glow of a new day. The world smelt clean and fresh from an earlier downpour, and all the birds were singing. Carter sat in the Land Rover parked at the front of the farm yard. His SMG and webbing belt were in the passenger seat, and he lounged back, bored out of his head. He had finished his book about half an hour ago, and was cursing himself for not bringing a second one with him when he'd known he was near the end.

Carter was thinking about his life. Where it was going? He didn't anticipate anything getting better, and this job he was doing was shit. When he was in barracks he did nothing but menial tasks, such as earth lugs, changing fuses, cleaning, guard duties, and drinking. On exercise, he was sitting in the back of the wagon for twelve hours a day - again, guard duty, eating, drinking. This wasn't the adventure he'd been sold. Then there were the blokes: he did not get on with his roommates, and most of the troop was offish with him. Then there was just about everything that happened around him. These people lived an alien world. This was not what he had expected.

He glanced at his watch: it was six o'clock. The sun had

now fully broken the horizon and it looked like being a pleasant summer day. It was another hour before he came off the guard duty, but as nothing ever happened at this time of the morning, he did not know why they bothered to put a guard out. They were neutral, so not part of the combat exercise, and no-one was going to attack them. Then suddenly a Land Rover pulled up at the entrance. Carter got out of his own vehicle and went over to see who it was; he was not expecting anyone, and as far as he knew no-one had left the compound.

"Who the fuck are you?" came a growl from the passenger seat.

"Corporal Carter! And who are you?"

The passenger suddenly opened the door, got out and walked round to the front of the Land Rover. "Staff Sergeant Green, Corporal!" he barked. Carter gave him a quick look up and down. The boots were highly polished and the perfectly fitting uniform was pressed into sharp creases in exactly the right places. Green was a short stocky man, with red hair, a small mouth, and deep-set beady eyes in a pale freckled face – and just now that face was snarling at Carter. "Where's your rifle, Soldier?"

"In the Land Rover, Staff!"

"And what the fuck is it doing in there? And what the fuck were *you* doing in there?"

"It was raining earlier, and I thought ...."

"You fucking thought, did you? You fucking did not want to get fucking wet, did you?" Green snarled, his face reddening. "Well, you fucking get your rifle and your webbing, and stand at the front of this yard like you're supposed to. When do you finish your guard?"

"Seven, Staff."

"Then at seven you come and find me and we will have a chat, Corporal!"

With that, Staff Green got back in his Land Rover, the driver smirking at Carter as they pulled into the yard. Somewhat sheepishly, Carter got out his rifle and webbing and made his way to the front of the farm-yard compound. Things could *not* get any worse, he thought to himself. The first meeting with Staff Green, and he was totally in the wrong and looked like a jerk. He imagined the sort of things Micky would have said to Staff Green, and now this. Carter had a bad feeling about all of it - and what a weazly looking man Green was! Hardly the warm, cosy sort either. No wonder his wife was out playing around.

Carter was relieved by Jenkins, who seemed - predict-ably enough - quite pleased to have heard that Carter was in the shit with Staff Green. He arrived to take over the guarding of the compound slightly earlier than the seven am change over, and with a snide smile on his face. "Green is livid with you, Carter. He hates Techs at the best of times, but you....! He really seems to have it in for you!"

Carter just nodded and made his way to the switch ve-hicle to find out where Staff Green would be. Tam was in there looking sympathetic, and with a freshly made cup of tea. "Don't worry, son! His bark is worse than his bite. Just keep your head down."

"Do you know where I can find him?"

"Yeah, he's in the command vehicle behind us."

"Cheers!"

Carter made sure his webbing was done up and that he had his rifle with him. He made his way down the steps of the switch, and then up the steps of the command vehicle. Staff Green was sitting on one of the stools inside with a bacon sandwich in his hand. "Did you fucking knock, Corporal?" he snapped. Carter shook his head. "Then get the fuck out and knock on the door before you come in here!"

He turned around, went outside again, shut the door, and then knocked. There was no answer. 'Tosser!' he thought. He knew this was going to be fun. After a minute or so he knocked again and waited.

This time he heard Green ask him to enter. Carter opened the door and stepped in.

"Carter, I have *not* heard a lot good things about you," he began, leaning back in his chair. "Bit flash, bit above his station, bit arrogant."

Carter looked down at Green sitting there. Where had he heard all that, if not from Micky! Toz was out on his radio relay wagon, so he couldn't have had the chance to speak to *him* yet.

"Well? What have you got to say for yourself, Carter?"

"Nothing, Staff."

"What was all that this morning with the Land Rover? You didn't want to get yourself all wet in the rain? Are you a bit of a fag, Carter?"

"No, Staff."

"Well, I think you *are*! I think you're a bum bandit fag. You going to prove otherwise?"

Carter said nothing. Not really the man management he was expecting.

"I am now going to punish you. This compound is

looking like shit. I want you to make sure there's no litter anywhere, and for every piece of litter I find, you will do ten press ups. Now fuck off out of my sight and get this compound cleaned up, you fag!"

"Yes, Staff." Carter turned and left the wagon. This is getting worse, he thought to himself, trying not to worry, trying desperately to think of a way out.

He made his way to the shed with the cookhouse in it, hit as he went in by the heat and the smell of frying food. The tent was filled with about ten lads already tucking into their fried breakfast. The big screen was showing the usual, but this morning the lads seemed not to be paying any attention. Carter got his breakfast from the sweating cook Micky, and then sat at a table with a couple of lads he still hadn't got to know. They looked at him, but without saying anything. Then shortly afterwards Green came in and made his way over to get his breakfast. Looking around the table as he passed, he spotted one of the lads not wearing his cam cream. "Barker, why are you not wearing your cam cream?" he barked.

"Just got up, and having my breakfast before I have a wash, Staff."

"Put your cam cream on!"

"I will after I've had a wash, Staff. I'm having a wash after my breakfast."

"Just do it now, Corporal, and stop whingeing!"

The corporal got his cam stick out of his webbing, spat into his hand and then mixed some cam before smearing it on his face. He quickly took a couple more mouthfuls of breakfast, and then got up to go and have a wash. Carter finished his food as quickly as he could without looking like he was rushing. Meanwhile, Green went and sat down with one of the groups of lads and started asking them how things were going.

Carter went back to the switch vehicle, where he found Tam and Beany on shift. "You're supposed to be off shift with your head down, Carter," commented Tam.

"Will do in a while. Just getting over the meeting with Staff Green."

"Yeah, we know - he was in here a while ago; doesn't seem to like you. He and Micky were good mates: he was the one that helped him get on the tech course. What did you do to Micky in Tech Training?"

"Nothing! I didn't really have anything to do with him. He just didn't seem to like me."

"Well, it looks like you upset Micky on that course, and that's why Green's got it in for you."

Carter tried to think back to Catterick. He hadn't hung out with Micky there; the only thing he could think of was that because he found the course easy and Micky struggled, he'd been asked to help him with his studies. Micky had said he did not want any help, and only just managed to scrape through, but at least he wasn't kicked off, like six others.

"I am sure it will pass." Carter tried to convince himself.

"For your sake, let's hope so!" said Tam.

Carter made his way over to the main shed where the sleeping accommodation was. As he walked towards the barn he could see a couple of the lads leaving and throwing bits of paper on the ground. This is really very childish, he thought, but picked the bits up and put them in his pocket, aware of Green's eyes on him as he walked through the dining area. He found his camp bed and stripping down to his t-shirt and underwear climbed into his sleeping bag. At first he pulled his rifle in with him, but finding it uncomfortable he moved it to under the bed and went to sleep.

***

Waking a number of hours later, Carter looked at his watch; it was just after four in the afternoon. He rubbed his eyes and leant under his bed to retrieve his rifle. It was gone. Moving his hand around he tried to locate it, then got out of his sleeping bag to have a look. No, the rifle was missing. Shit! he thought to himself. If things could get any worse....! He got up, put on his combats and webbing belt and made way to the wash area. As stood washing his face, someone walked up to him. "Missing something, Carter?" Carter just turned and nodded. "Staff Green wants to see you in the command wagon."

Carter said nothing, just finished washing, brushed his teeth, put on his cam cream and made his way to the command vehicle. He knocked on the door and waited for an answer, and then someone called him in. There were three people in the wagon: Lieutenant Harrington and his Foreman, Staff Gant, as well as Staff Green. "One of yours, Foreman! Didn't like the rain this morning and now he's lost his rifle!" Green stated. Carter looked at the three with nothing to say.

"What shall we do with him? It's not been a day yet, and he's come to my attention twice already, plus I have a handful of litter here, and it was his task to keep the compound clear of rubbush. Not a good start Carter," he went on, "and this is your first time in the field. What have you got to say for yourself?"

Carter paused, thinking about what to say but knowing whatever he did say would be shot down. "Sitting in the Land Rover was an oversight of mine...."

"Fucking oversight! What oversight was that then, Soldier?" Green barked. Carter was silent, at a loss for what to say. "Come on! Over fucking sight! What is this, a fucking committee meeting? You're in the Army now, Carter, and from what's happened so far I'd say you have a bit of catching up and growing up to do!"

Satff Gant interjected. "The loss of weapon is a chargeable offence, but I will let it go this time"

"No you fucking won't!"

"Yes we will, Staff Sergeant!" Gant snapped back. "Remember your place here! I am senior here, and this is *my* man under *my* command. As for the guard this morning, Carter, I am putting you on double guard duties. You're on shift with Jenkins so you can do his, as well as your own. You come to our attention again and I will really have to sort something out with you, Corporal."

"There's still the litter!" Green snapped. "I have twelve pieces here. That's 120 press ups."

"That's your issue, Staff Sergeant, to be dealt with in your own manner. Now Carter, you'd best screw the nut in and get on with being a soldier." With that Staff Gant left the command vehicle to go to the technical maintenance wagon.

"Right! Come with me, and we'll get those press ups done."

With Green leading the way, he and Carter made their way to the shed and found a suitable corner. "Now Carter," he snarled," get down and push them out – one hundred and twenty!" Carter went to take his webbing belt off. "*No* Carter, webbing belt *ON*!" The belt adding a few pounds to his weight, he got into the prone position and began his press ups, with Green counting them out. "Chest to the floor! That one didn't count – AGAIN!"

By the ninetieth press up his arms were on fire and he could feel the muscles begin to cramp, but he kept at it. Staring fixedly at the floor, he willed himself to go on pushing up and down. Then, when at last he reached 120, Green suddenly lashed out and kicked him hard in the waist, winding him. "That's for losing your fucking weapon, Cunt! And don't expect any more protection from Staff Gant either. You're in *my* troop, and I will have you, you cunt! Now get up, and get out of my sight!" And with that, he turned and walked off. Carter pulled himself off the floor. His arms burned and he was trying to get his breath back. He made his way back to the main barn and sat and had a coffee, watching a woman entertain a black man with her arse. Did they never turn this shit off! he groaned to himself.

Staff Sergeant Green sat in the command vehicle on his own, looking about him: six phones connected to the sides of the wagon over a bench that ran around the vehicle, with paperwork on the bench desk attached to the side of the vehicle itself. There were six stools like the one he sat on. Green was thirty-six years old. He had joined the Army as a boy soldier and had gone to Harrogate to train to be a technician, but had failed the course in the second year; his maths and logic were not up to it. As it turned out, though, that had not had been the end, but the start of his career. In Junior Troop he had made it to the rank of RSM. As a soldier he was good: he liked to keep things neat, loved drill, loved weapons and cleaning them, loved the discipline. Having reached the rank of RSM, when he got to Catterick he had been put forward for Junior Leaders, which was the pre-assessment for becoming an officer, but once again his education had let him down, so he trained to be a radio relay operator. It had taken him sixteen years to become a Staff Sergeant.

In that time the Army had changed. The training had got softer, the soldiers had got softer, the physical training had got softer, and he had no idea where it was all going. He had just six years left to do before his pension, but he could see that six years being slow. The likes of Carter made it slow. These kids were turning up from training with no discipline and no backbone, and there was nothing he could do about it. The days were gone when he could take a kid round the back of the shed and kick the living crap out of him until that kid had the fear in him that if he did anything at all wrong he would get another kicking. He had known this Carter less than a day, and he had lost his weapon and didn't want to get wet. Lost a weapon – Jesus! What if he'd done that in his early years?

Looking down at his well-polished boots, he decided there and then that he was going to turn Carter into a soldier. He was in *his* troop: it *was* his – he was the Troop Commander!, the young Lieutenant Harrington did what he was told, he was just doing his stint until he made Captain and got a good desk job.

Carter was his.

Chapter 8

Carter was glad to fire up the engine of the four-tonner. It had been a hard two weeks since Staff Green had come to the node, and he had been run ragged. The litter thing had turned into a joke, with him pushing out press ups every day since. Then there was the run for this; fetch that; I want you to drive me here, drive me there. He'd tried to make conversation with Green, but Green hadn't wanted to talk. As he sat there with him in the Land Rover, either going to pick up supplies or visit a radio relay location his mind drifted to Ingrid. Green had no idea what his wife was up to, or if he did, he was in denial. Carter thought about all the shit Green was giving him, and promised himself the next time he saw his wife he was not going to hold back. He would take out on her what Green was taking out on him.

Tam jumped into the passenger seat. "Bet you're glad to be getting back to camp! You should be able to find somewhere to hide from Green there. Green by name, green by nature!"

"Fuck it! He's really got it in for me," moaned Carter. "Don't know what to do."

"Just try and keep your head down," Tam lit a cigarette, "and stop fucking up. Losing your weapon, not cleaning your boots! You're making yourself a target. When the next new boy arrives the heat will come off you." Carter looked down at Tam's filthy boots and his own well-polished ones, but said nothing. He couldn't wait to get back to camp, get in that shower and call Lemska to see if she wanted to go out.

The drive back to barracks was a lot quicker, as they were allowed to use the motorways. The four- tonner managed to maintain just over 55mph. Tam was all smiles, looking forward to getting home to his wife and little boy. It was still early evening when they pulled into the barracks, but a couple of the other troops had arrived before them, and there was a lot activity around the vehicles already parked up. They had to be ready for inspection - cleaned, replenished and ready to go out immediately if required, in case World War Three broke out at a moment's notice.

Two hours later Tam was locking up the back of the switch after it had been inspected by Sergeant Bickerstaff. "Hang the keys in the troop office, and that's us done for the next three days!" The regiment had been given the Monday off and the weekend was theirs. The next parade was six am Tuesday for a run. Carter walked up to the squadron block with Jenkins, who still wouldn't talk to Carter. Once he got to his room after hanging up the keys to the switch, he was happy to see that Toz, Lenny and Mark were not back yet. Stripping off, he made his way to the showers. Jonah was already there with Barker, another technician who had been in the troop for a few years, but was very quiet and kept himself to himself. There was something about Barker that meant everyone left him be. He was not the typical soldier; he was not the typical human being. He was biding his time, and he had a plan.

"Hi Carter! How did your first exercise go?" asked Jonah as Carter joined them in the row of showers. "Oh, as good as that!" he laughed, seeing his face. Barker finished his shower, dried himself off and left the room without saying a word.

"You fancy going out tonight?"

"I'm going to phone that Lemska girl and see what she's up to"

"Well, if she's busy, come down to Café Wichtig. All the boys will be down there and it's a real riot, but something you need to see. Plus, I think you could do with some introductions. It seems you're a bit of a scapegoat at the moment."

"Tell me about it! Green's got it in for me big time. You'd think I'd shagged his wife or something!"

"Don't joke, mate! If he knew, he'd fucking kill you! He overheard someone just talking about his wife a year or so ago and put the guy in hospital. He had to have his jaw re-wired."

"Shit! He must know what she's like."

"No, he doesn't - even though about four lads in this regiment have had her, and God knows how many Tankies and guys from 7 Sigs."

"He's bound to find out sooner or later."

"You just don't want to be the guy in the hot seat when he does!

"You had her then, Jonah?"

"Yeah, in his bed in their quarters! He's always away on courses being a Super Soldier. I was pissed, and she's very convincing. Fucked her all weekend until she was sore, if you know what I mean."

Carter finished his shower and they both agreed to go down the Pigs' Bar as soon as they changed.

He had never called a number outside the UK before, and the ring tone was different from what he was used to: a long ring, a pause, a long ring. The phone was answered with, "Lemska, bitte!" then there was some German spoken on the receiving end.

"Hello! Is that Lemska? It's me, Chris! We met a couple of weeks ago at the Go-Park."

"Chris! Hi Chris! You back from your exercise, yes?"

"Yes, and I was wondering what you're doing tonight."

"It is a bit late, Chris. It is eight-thirty - too late to go out!" Carter suddenly realised it *was* late.

"Ok, sorry! I have the whole weekend free, though. How about tomorrow?" The beeps on the pay phone rang in his ear, and he put another Deutsche Mark in the slot.

"I can see you tomorrow evening if you would like. I finish work at five, so we can meet around seven. Where would you like to meet?"

"I don't know. Herford, somewhere?" Carter suggested.

"How about I pick you up at your barracks and we start from there?"

"Sounds like a good plan. I will be outside the barracks at seven."

"Ok, see you tomorrow!" and Lemska hung up the phone just as he was about to say something back.

Smiling to himself, Carter made his way to find Jonah in the Pigs' Bar.

***

Staff Sergeant Alan Green unlatched the gate to his front lawn and made his way up the path to the door, but a smiling Ingrid had opened it before he got there. Behind her legs stood a little boy of five and half, with dark hair and a fair complexion like his mother's. When he saw his father, he ran out in excitement, calling, "Daddy, Daddy, Daddy!" Al Green dropped his heavy Bergen onto the grass so that he could pick up his son and hug him. "Shouldn't you be in bed, Sunny Jim?" he asked, looking at his watch. It was twenty past nine, but the little boy shook his head.

"He's been trying to stay awake all night, waiting for his daddy to come home." Ingrid smiled at the little boy.

Al took his son into the living room and put him on the sofa; then went back and retrieved his Bergen, leaving it in the hall. He sat down on the sofa next to Matthew and ruffled his hair. Ingrid came into the room with a cold glass of beer which Al finished in one and Ingrid took the glass out to re fill. Matthew's head was lolling against his father's side and his eyelids were beginning to look heavy. Al let the child drift off with his arm around him while he sipped a second beer a bit more slowly. "I'm really looking forward to a nice warm soapy bath, and having this long weekend off." He smiled at Ingrid. "Do you fancy jumping in the car and going to find somewhere to visit?"

"Sounds good to me. Let me take Matthew up to bed now. He must be exhausted. He was already drifting in and out of sleep a couple of hours ago – I'm surprised he made it to see you home!"

Al ruffled Matthew's hair as Ingrid picked him up to take him upstairs to bed, then sat back on the sofa and switched on the TV. There was only one English channel to watch on BFBS TV, but sometimes the German channels put on an English film, or transmitted one with subtitles. He flicked up and down the options, and then switched the TV off and put the CD cassettes on random play on the hi-fi. Ingrid came back in with a glass of wine. "Matthew is down and I've set the bath running." She sat down next to her husband and gave him a kiss on the lips. Al smiled at her, kissing her again and Ingrid got up, saying, "I'll check your bath and call you up when it is ready."

A while later he heard his name being called and made his way upstairs with his beer. He stripped off in the bedroom, went to the bathroom, climbed into the warm bubbly water and let his head rest against the back of the bath. Ingrid went down for another beer, then into the bedroom, and came back wearing a see-through nightie. Well aware of Al becoming aroused at the sight of her body through the flimsy fabric, Ingrid smiled and sat on the closed toilet seat with her wine. They talked for half an hour while Al Green soaked. Once he was finished in the bath Ingrid dried him off, then took him to bed and they made love.

***

Carter's head hurt as he lay on his bed staring at the ceiling, trying to recall what had happened the night before. He took a look around the room and could see Mark, but Toz and Lenny were missing. He turned to his right and saw his clothes in a pile by his bed. He tried to think back to last night but could not recall getting back to his room, or most of the night itself.

Jonah was right! The Café Wichtig had been a riot: it was the roughest place Carter had ever been in - a proper spit and sawdust sort of place. The Pigs' Bar was bad enough, but here glasses built up on the tables, cigarettes in ashtrays, and the staff made no attempt to come out from behind the bar to tidy up. The punters sat around drinking and smoking and listening to the DJ. The club was frequented exclusively by English soldiers, there were no local lads. The girls were all local, and had come there specifically to meet and be entertained by English soldiers.

Carter remembered being in the dance floor part of the night club sitting on a bench along one wall, with a floor to ceiling mirror opposite. The mirror was made of very highly polished metal: if it had been glass, it wouldn't have lasted a night. Quite a few of the soldiers danced with each other, not in a gay way, but in a drunken boogie way, and others danced in a group with some of the few girls in the place. There must have been about ten girls to the two hundred plus soldiers.

There were a few fights, but not anything serious; some of the lads just liked to fight. One of them was sitting in a corner showing anyone who was interested how he liked to burn his pubic hair with his lighter. One of the competitions was to hold a nearly finished cigarette between your arm and your opponent's, and whoever pulled away first bought the next round. Then there was the puking up game: whoever was last in the group to puke had to pick up a lump of vomit from the floor and eat it. Most of the lads just seemed to want to get as drunk as they could, and weren't really interested in the women in the club. Those that were, took turns at buying them drinks and having a grope. Carter remembered hearing one of the girls entertaining someone in a cubicle when he went to the bathroom. He was not planning on going back there any time soon!

He pulled himself out of bed and made his way to the shower. He was meeting Lemska tonight, so he planned to have breakfast, go for a nice long run for an hour or so, have lunch, and then read a novel until it was time for tea. He was really looking forward to seeing Lemska, so he knew the day would drag.

***

At five to seven Carter stood by the main road outside the barrack gates waiting for Lemska to arrive. He had already been there ten minutes kicking his heels against the kerb, and he had no idea what car she was driving, so watched every one that passed. Then, just a minute after seven a silver Audi 80 pulled up. Carter leant down and looked in, and there was Lemska in the driving seat in a summery dress and with a smile on her face. Carter opened the door and got in the passenger side.

"Hi there!" smiled Lemska. "Where do you fancy going then, Mr Carter?"

"Don't mind- haven't given it a thought! Remember I'm a new boy here!" Carter smiled back.

"Well leave it to me then, I know somewhere we can go."

After about half an hour of driving and chatting, Lemska pulled up outside an old looking tavern. When they walked in the barman greeted Lemska by name, and then led them over to a table by the window. The tavern walls were hung with pictures of mountain and country scenes and the general ambience of the place was what might be described as Old World Germany. A waiter came over with a jug of water and a menu each for Lemska and Carter. The menu was written all in German and Carter had no idea what was what. Lemska ordered a bottle of wine and the waiter left them.

"Can you read German, Chris?" Lemska asked.

Carter shook his head.

"Do you like meat or vegetables? What do you like to eat?"

"I really don't mind, but I do like to explore food, so I will leave it up to your recommendation." Lemska smiled at this. Carter liked her smile; she was fresh faced with blue-green eyes, and her hair was light brown, close to mousy. This was the first time since he had arrived in Germany that things felt normal.

The wine, a slightly sweet Riesling, was brought over and Lemska waited for Carter to try it. He knew what to do; he had been out with his parents and their friends in the past and watched his father taste wine many times. He thought with satisfaction that Lemska seemed quietly to approve of his savoir faire as she watched him. "I thought I would order an easy German white and we shall have a full German meal." She smiled and ordered a number of dishes from the menu

"So what do you do, Lemska?" Carter asked.

"I work for my father. He is businessman and I work for one of his companies."

"Doing what?"

"Well, my father believes in working your way up, so I started on Reception. I have a degree in modern history, but Father said if I want to work with him, it is not a gift and I have to earn my way to a useful level of competency. At the moment I'm doing his book keeping."

"Sounds a bit tough!"

"Father started from nothing, and he's sixty-five now. He joined a Panzer unit when he was eighteen, and was twenty-one when the war finished. The barracks you are in now, that was the barracks his regiment came from. After the war there was nothing, and now he runs four different companies, operating in different areas of business." Lemska was obviously proud of her father.

"So your dad was a Nazi in the war?"

Lemska frowned. "No, he was not a Nazi. He *had* to join, but he was not a soldier by inclination. It was what you were compelled to do in those days. The war was on the turn when he had to join in 1942. He said he was lucky to do battle with the softer, European troops, at the end of the war and not still be on the Eastern Front."

"Fascinating! Never thought of it on the other side of the coin. My grandfather was 8th Army from the start of the war until the end - a D Day Dodger and all that. He was conscripted when the war started because he was unemployed. He was one of only a few that survived the whole stint with the 8th."

"I think my dad was at Monte Casino - they could have been either side of the battle line! Anyway, he worked hard to get where he is today, and he wants me to do the same."

"Any brothers and sisters?"

"One brother. He's away travelling at the moment. Father hates it, but he accepts Ralf has to find his own way."

The first course arrived - cabbage soup. Carter tried it, and pretended to like it, even though it wasn't really to his taste!

"So what do you think of Germany?" Lemska asked.

"I haven't really seen any of it. I've been stuck in a farmyard slightly north of here for six weeks. I've been for runs and around the barracks area and into town, but that's about it."

Lemska smiled, "Well, if you like, I would be happy to show you around a bit of Germany."

Carter smiled back. "Yes, I'd like that!" and they toasted each other as the next course arrived. It was a selection of sausages with sauerkraut, and various meats, Lemska explaining each dish as they worked their way through. They both had dessert, and after the meal she insisted on paying the bill. Carter tried to protest, but Lemska was having none of it. "Well, you must let me next time!" he exclaimed.

"Yes, next time, but I thought soldiers didn't get paid very much?" Lemska smiled again.

"Well yes, you're right. But I'm not skint! I can pay my own way."

"Don't worry! My treat. You're a nice man and I like your company."

They got up and made their way back to her car. Carter stood by the driver's door and opened it for her, then made his way round to the passenger seat. As they pulled out of the car park to drive back to the barracks Lemska put some music on the radio cassette player. It was the German group, Propaganda, and Carter recognised one of the songs that had been a hit in the UK in the early eighties.

"You like German music?"

"I listen to anything. If I like it, I like it"

"So why are you in the Army, Chris? You don't seem to be like any of the other Army men I meet around here."

"You met many then?"

"A few, yes, but only a couple through meeting them in the club, and they were just horrible. You are very relaxed and kind. You have been pleasant all evening, and don't seem to be someone who just wants to sleep with me."

"Tell me about it! The whole set up here has been a real shock to my system. Training was ok, but since I've been here..... well, it's just madness. It's boring, the lads are all a bit off the wall, and the job is rubbish"

"So how did you end up joining? You volunteered, yes?"

"Short of it is, my parents divorced. I was supposed to go to university, but due to the divorce and wrangling over money I couldn't afford it. I was walking past an Army recruiting office in Romford one weekend and thought it would be a good way to escape and go on an adventure. The Recruiting Sergeant convinced me I could get a trade and a career I could use in Civvy

Street when I got out. "Just sign up for six to nine years," he said. "Nine is better because you get more money. You'll still be under thirty when you come out, and highly employable. My dad was in the Royal Engineers during National Service and it didn't seem to do him any harm, so I joined."

"And you don't like it?"

"Not at the moment. But it's still early days. I probably just need to get used to it."

They turned into the road where the barracks was, and Lemska pulled the car up a little way short of the barracks. "Thank you, Lemska. I really enjoyed that meal - and your company. I would like to see you again," said Carter.

"I also. How would you like to meet tomorrow and we can go for a nice walk? We Germans like our walks on a Sunday!"

"I'd love that!" and Carter leant over and gave Lemska a kiss before getting out of the car.

"I'll pick you up at ten tomorrow, then, at the same place," and she drove off, waving happily.

Carter smiled to himself as he made his way back to his room. That was the first normal day he'd had since arriving at 4th Armoured Division.

***

Next morning Carter again found himself standing on the road outside the barracks waiting for Lemska. Twice in two days. Did he like her, or was he just keen to get out of the barracks! Probably both. When he got back to his room the previous night, Toz, Lenny and Mark were drinking and watching pornography *again*.

You would have thought they'd get bored with it eventually. This film was slightly different from the usual. It was shot by a hand held camera, and was about a man picking up girls off the street or in bars, getting them a bit drunk and then taking them back to a room where a number of his friends were waiting. Then the girl would either accept her fate, or be brutally gang raped. God knows where this film came from, but Toz had borrowed it off someone who'd got it on a trip to Amsterdam. Now it was doing the rounds, Animal Farm having lost its appeal in comparison.

Carter had put on his headphones, and lay on his bed reading a book. Then at about eight Toz and his crew set off for a night out, leaving him in peace. Jonah had come in a little while later, but Carter told him he was staying in for the night. After a bit of small talk, he explained that he wouldn't be going for a run in the morning because he was meeting Lemska. Jonah smiled and left him to his book, The Destroyer by Warren Murphy/ Richard Sapir, and AC/DC's 'Powerage' on his headphones. After the meal with Lemska and discovering her father had been in a tank regiment, he was planning to read Sven Hassel again.

Toz, Lenny and Mark came in again at about two with a couple of drunken girls. They spent some time showing the girls their new video, and then taking turns with each of them. Carter lay low with his back to them, but one of the girls came over and asked why he didn't want to join in. He feigned sleep, trying his hardest to block them out, and then heard Toz tell the girl to ignore him - he was gay. Waking early next morning, he went for a run at about six, having struggled to sleep through the sound of springs and moans. They just didn't lay off, and it was gone four before they started to calm down. When he left the room he saw that one of the girls had passed out on the sofa, and the other one was with Mark on his bed. After his run he had a shower then breakfast, but the girls were still there when he left to meet Lemska. Lenny was awake, but there was little sign of life from the others.

Lemska's car pulled up just before ten, and she smiled happily as Carter got in. She was wearing a loose-fitting white shirt, flared jeans, and a long, coloured necklace. Her face looked fresh, with only a hint of make-up. They drove for about forty minutes before pulling into a large car park in some woods. There were a lot of people around, with walking shoes, walking sticks and rucksacks. "I told you we Germans like our Sunday walks!" Lemska opened the boot and took out a small rucksack "I've brought us a packed lunch and a blanket," she smiled. "Here - you take it!"

On the opposite side of the car park at the entrance to the wood was a large board with a map marked with different coloured routes. "These are the various walks, and the time they take," explained Lemska. "You pick a colour and it shows the time. We're going to do the blue walk today; it circles the lake, and takes about two hours." Carter smiled as they set off down the trail, following the blue markers. The weather was perfect, the sun was out, and he couldn't think of a better way to spend a Sunday.

After following the blue route through the cool woods for about forty minutes, the path suddenly opened out to reveal the lake, surrounded by woodland but edged with a grassy bank. Lemska led Carter onto the grass and they walked about ten minutes away from the path into a secluded area overlooking the water. He took off the rucksack and Lemska got out a small blanket and laid it on the ground. She unpacked a couple of glasses and some plates and started laying out their lunch. "Are you hungry? I also have a bottle of wine. This time it is French, and Chardonnay." They both sat on the blanket and Carter looked out across the lake. The water was like glass; in the distance he could see people walking along the path.

"This is lovely!" said Carter dreamily.

Lemska smiled as she put sandwiches and salad on the plates and passed Carter the bottle of wine and an opener. The wine was sweet on his lips as they toasted each other, and then Lemska sat back on the blanket.

They spent the next twenty minutes eating and talking about the food - cold meat and sausage, Sauerkraut, mayonnaise and coleslaw. After the meal Carter lay back on the blanket letting his face soak up the sun, and Lemska did the same. They lay there in silence for a few minutes before Lemska said, "What a shame we cannot capture these moments and live with them forever! The peace and the happiness we feel now, the perfect weather, the sound of nature around us, and no complications of knowing the bad things about each other."

Carter sighed as he looked up at the sky and listened to the sounds of the lake, the buzz of nature all around him. "Yes, it is a shame! Because when all's said and done, the world is definitely *not* a peaceful, happy place to be….."

Chapter 9

The morning air was cold and Carter could feel goose bumps on his arms. It was 08:00hrs on Tuesday morning. After Carter's relaxing afternoon with Lemska on the Sunday, he had cheerfully waved her off when she dropped him at the barracks just before six. He got back to find Jonah in his room and they'd gone to the Naafi together, rented a video and bought a Herfy handbag. After the film and a few beers Carter had retired to bed.

On Monday morning he went for his usual six o'clock run. Toz and the crew had not returned to the room on Sunday night, but they appeared Monday afternoon looking pleased with themselves. Lenny had brought in a video recorder and they bragged about how much cash they had lifted. From what Carter could gather, they'd been taken back to some woman's house on the Sunday, spent the night with her, then left while she was still sleeping, helping themselves to the video recorder and whatever cash she had in her bag. Carter had gone out for most of the rest of the day, walking in the woods and finding a quiet tavern where he could read and have a couple of beers.

On the Tuesday morning the squadron had paraded in sports gear at 06:00hrs and had been split into groups.

These were a fast group, a medium group and the slow runners, which was where all the older soldiers were, together with Staff Gant and his sergeants from the basement. Carter was put in the fast group, which also included Staff Green. After a forty minute run Carter made sure he beat Staff Green back to barracks on the sprint in. He beat him easily, letting Green get up to his shoulder and then left him for the last half a mile. Green was not happy.

The Parade was called to attention. Staff Sergeant Green and Sergeant Bickerstaff stood at the front of Panther Troop. The rest of the squadron stood in its troops in rows of three. One Squadron 4ADSR was made up of Panther and Cheetah Troops, both being housed in the first floor of the block with troop offices side by side. Staff Green read out the roll call to answers of "Present!" There were no gaps this time, but on numerous occasions someone would be missing. They were given twenty-four hours to appear before being reported as AWOL. This was to allow them to find their way back to barracks after a heavy weekend, or to sober up and return if they had thought it was a good idea to do a runner.

There were two cars in the car park, though, that had been there for quite a while! Nipper Smith had been the Squadron Boxing Champ and on a boxing tour of the UK when he decided it would be a good time to do a runner. He hadn't been seen since. When you went AWOL the MPs checked your parents, girlfriends and some friends' houses but not a lot more. They waited for you to appear somewhere with your national insurance number, or in hospital or a police station.

If captured, you would be made to do your time in Colchester nick, or the Military Corrective Training Centre (MCTC), also known as the Glass House. This was the central Army prison where you would be sent for corrective training if you broke the law in the Military. It was like basic training but a bit more intense. For some guys it had been the start of an illustrious career. Not only had they been "corrected" they had also completed a number of courses while serving their time, and then shot up the ranks by virtue of the skills they learnt there. Those who didn't want their parents to know they had been sent to a hard correction jail told them they were on a six months' training course.

Lieutenant Harrington now joined the parade, marching up to Staff Green and saluting. He was told everyone was present and correct. He then read out some information about current affairs and news of the Regiment and its forthcoming activities, and told them the recent exercise had been a successful one. He revealed that there had been shifts in the state of the Russian Government, and warned them to keep an eye out for UVBT's (Under Vehicle Booby Traps). The IRA were known to be active in Germany again and looking for soft targets. It had not been that long since there had been a shooting of a soldier on the German/ Dutch border.

At this point, Staff Green took over. Carter heard his name being called out to be placed on Guard Detail for the next two weeks. Green also ordered him to come and see him in his office after the parade.

After fifteen minutes the parade finished and everyone moved off to begin their work for the day. The radio relay crews went off to their wagons to carry out maintenance, the technicians went down to the basement to get their daily assignments from Staff Gent, and Carter made his way to the Troop Office. When he walked in Staff Green was already behind his desk, and the Troop Officer at his. Carter came to a halt and saluted. Staff Green looked at Carter. "You can have the day off, Carter; you are now on Guard Duty tonight. It is a two week rota. You do a week of nights and a week of days. You need to report to the guard room at seven pm tonight in combat dress."

That was all that was said. Carter saluted Lieutenant Harrington, who was sitting at the other desk, did an about-turn and then made his way to his room. He had a day of nothing to do. Lying back on his bed, he pulled a book down from his shelf and started to read, and before long – with a break for lunch and tea - the day had passed.

***

Shortly before seven Carter made his way to the Guard Room situated close to the front gate. There were a number of soldiers standing outside, all dressed in the same combats. It was a pleasant evening and most of the guys stood about smoking and chatting. At just on seven a corporal came out and called parade. The soldiers formed into two lines for inspection, and a sergeant and an officer came out of the Guard Room. The officer was a Second Lieutenant and looked no older than nineteen. The sergeant called the squad to attention, and both men made their way up and down the lines, inspecting for the smartness of the guard. When asked for his ID card by the sergeant, Carter reached in his back pocket for his wallet. "Shame, Soldier!" rapped the sergeant. "I should be giving you stick man, but for your ID not being in your top left pocket where it is supposed to be!" The sergeant and the officer moved on. Carter was gutted. Stick man is where you are best dressed soldier of the guard and you get to go back to your room on standby in case anything happens, and nothing ever happens, but you get to have the night off rather than do stags all night. After the office and sergeant had inspected the squad they called out Pearson as the stick man and he was relieved of his duty. With a smile and a "Stag on, bastards!" he was off to his room with a skip and a jump.

"Carter and Barker, you're on the gate first!" the corporal shouted. "Go in the Guard Room and get your weapons! Lawlor, you are VCP (Vehicle Check Point); the rest of you, get in the back and sort yourselves out!" Carter made for the Guard room, where he was issued an SLR rifle with thirty rounds of 7.62, which he was to put in his ammo pouch on his webbing; the rifle itself was to have an empty magazine attached. Once he had the weapon, he made his way out to the sand bunker beside the Guard Room. Here he performed his safety drills with the weapon, to check it was clear of live rounds. He fitted the empty magazine, and then once Barker had done the same drill he made his way over to the gate. At that point two smiling faces went past them, their day on guard duty now over.

Barker stood on the opposite side from Carter and looked out onto the road. Carter did the same. They had to be out on guard for two hours, and two hours can drag. The routine for the next two weeks was: two hours' gate guard, one hour VCP, three hours' rest, and two hours' gate guard; *or* two hours' gate guard, one hour's rest, one hour VCP, two hours' rest, two hours gate guard - and on and on.

The job was to check everyone's passes when they entered the barracks; if they were in a car, the car was checked at the VCP for bombs. There was a current threat from the IRA, and in the past they had held someone's family hostage and made one of them drive a bomb into the barracks. This happened a few years ago in JHQ Rheindahlen, when a high ranking office had had his house broken into. The bomb was discovered by the VCP on same day and the family had been rescued. This was real, but a lot of the time it did not feel like it, and it always happened somewhere else. There had been a number of IRA incidents in recent years: a soldier had been shot in his car on the Dutch border, and an officer shot near his house in another part of Germany.

Carter stood at the gate, not feeling threatened or in danger. Ten minutes had gone by without a word from Barker, and not a soul had gone in or out of the gate. It was a Monday evening and not a lot was going on. An hour later Barker wanted to swap sides. He'd said nothing for the last half an hour, just stood at the gate silently watching the cars go by.

"I'm Chris. And you?"

"Colin," Barker told him.

"Where are you from?"

"Loughton, in Essex. You?"

"No shit! I'm from Debden, just down the road. Small world!"

"So you know Romford and Epping Forest and all that."

"Yeah, used to ride round Epping Forest on my bike all the summer," Carter smiled. "How long have you been here? Not seen you about."

"Too long - and I try to keep my head down."

"What trade are you? What troop?"

"I'm a technician with Panther Troop, same as you."

"No shit! Technician too! I've never seen you in the workshop, though."

"As I said, keeping my head down and just doing my time."

"Nice to meet you!"

"Likewise."

"So what do you think of it here?"

"Hate it! It's just not what I was led to expect. I hate my job, hate what it is all about, and this place seems to be running amok with male testosterone."

"How come I've never seen you about?"

"Keep myself to myself, and try to do as many of these guard duties as I can. Most guys will pay to have theirs done. It gives me money, keeps me out of the troop lines and away from bother, and gives me a day off every so often to do my own thing."

After another hour and half Carter had discovered he did not know anyone that Barker knew back home, even though they were only three years apart in age. Strange, he thought, how people may live within only a few miles of each other without ever crossing paths. It was now coming up to nine o'clock, and Barker asked,

"Do you fancy doing first VCP?"

"Don't mind."

"Thanks. I need a brew and a sit down."

The next gate guard relieved them: another two young-sters, who seemed to be good mates and had big smiles on their faces as they came out. Carter and Barker made their way to the sand pit and cleared their weap-ons before Carter reloaded his with the empty maga-zine and made his way outside to the front of the guard room. There was a row of six small traffic cones there, within which any car entering the barracks would have to stop. During the peak period of the morning between seven and nine there would be two bays, and you would both do a two hour VCO stint. At this time of night, though, nothing was coming in or out of the barracks. The lads would be in the bar and the married soldiers would have left for home at about four.

Carter stood looking at the dishevelled cones. He had nothing better to do than put them on parade, so he spent the next half an hour marshalling them into a straight line. It was dark now, the lights had gone on and he was alone with his thoughts. What was he go-ing to do, what sort of life lay ahead? Had he made a serious error of judgement in joining up?

After a little more than fifty minutes Barker came out to relieve him. Carter was pleased to see him, and they stood chatting for a minute.

"Nice line! Now what am *I* to do for the next hour?"

Carter walked over to the cones and kicked them all over.

"Put them on parade!"

Barker smiled. "Thanks Chris, I'll have them spick and

span! Now get yourself inside and have some sleep."

Carter thanked him and made his way to the guard room entrance. He was met by the Guard Corporal, and cleared his weapon in the sand box before going on in. The room itself was small, but with a big window facing out to the gate. On one wall was a large notice board with the Regimental Orders on it. The latest security posters were on the wall: Always Check the Underside of Your Car for UVBT; Don't Tell Secrets - You Don't Know Who is Listening'. Under this board was a row of radios and to the left was the rifle rack that held all the SLR rifles.

The corporal wore a webbing belt with a pistol holster that held a 9mm Browning. His name was Peterson, another technician from Mike Troop. He had been at the regiment for just over three years and had qualified for his T1 training. He made himself a coffee and asked the corporal if he wanted anything. The corporal said he would like a coffee. Carter made two coffees and took one over to Peterson. The corporal had dark curly hair and blue eyes; his face was pale and he looked like he could do with a good square meal.

"What do you think of it here, then?" he asked.

"Not really decided yet"

"Don't worry about being in the Relay Troop. I started there - bunch of animals! I got up to my T2 then I was moved to Mike Troop. Scored just under 100% and they decided I was wasted on earth lugs. A lot easier in Mike Troop, you know."

"Is this what you were expecting when you joined up?"

"Fuck no! I was *expecting* to be fixing kit, going on adventures, having fun."

"Not just me then. I got it all wrong too."

"Don't worry! - this is just a bad place. I know loads of guys that love what they're doing. Just do a stint here and get out. 4ADSR is renowned for being a shit hole. Did you do anything wrong in training? They tend to send the bad boys here."

"Not that I know of. Just unlucky I guess."

"More than that! I hear you get to share a room with Toz and his crew."

"Tell me about it!"

"Toz and Staff Green are thick as thieves, so just be careful there."

"I will. Anyway, I'm going to hit the sack for a bit. Nice to talk to you…?"

"Clive, my name's Clive. Nice to speak to you too, Chris - and don't let this place get you down."

Carter made his way to the back room, where there were eight beds. A TV and video player stood on a table in the corner, and – surprise, surprise! - there was a porn film playing. Carter tried to ignore it as he made his way to an empty bed and pulled a book out of his webbing: Lesley Thomas's Adventures of Goodnight and Loving. He felt like running away, but unlike the marriage in the book his vows had been made to the Army, and he was signed up for nine years. He gradually lost himself his book, and the moans and groans from the TV faded into the background.

***

He was awoken by a kick to the legs. "Wake up sleeping beauty!!" Barker was smiling as he stood over Carter's bed. He came to, opened his eyes, looked about the

118

room and then down at his watch. It was ten to midnight. "Have this coffee before we go out on the gate." Barker passed the coffee down, and Carter took a reviving sip.

Ten minutes later they were both on the gate. The road outside was silent, the sky was clear and the moon and stars were bright. It was not really cold, but there was an edge to the night air.

"What do you do on your days off?" asked Carter.

"Now that would be telling!" Barker smiled.

"What would be telling?"

"What I do on my days off."

"What are your plans then? Are you a long-termer? How come you joined up?"

"No I'm not a long-termer. As a tech, though, I had to sign for six or nine, and I went for the six, they tried to convince me on nine!"

"I know; I fell for the nine line…more money."

"Anyway, I'm planning to do my T1, do my second stint, and then get out at six year point. I'll still only be twenty four."

"That's a long fucking time though, six years."

"I've already done one and half years, so that's only four and a half to go."

"Go on, then! Tell me what you do on your days off!"

"Carter, you seem ok! - meet me here, outside the guard room at midday tomorrow and you'll see."

Chapter 10

At one pm next day Carter was standing just outside the entrance to the barracks. The guard had finished at 07:00hrs and he had gone straight to his bed. He managed to get to sleep once his roommates left to go on parade at eight. Then after sleeping through until twelve, he got up for a shower and grabbed some lunch from the cook house. His body was a bit out of kilter from the strange sleeping patterns, but he felt OK.

Barker drew up to the kerb in a blue convertible XR3i; it had British plates and looked brand new. "Nice car!" said Carter as he got in.

"Yep, and it's already sold for more than I bought it for." Barker smiled at the expression on Carter's face. "Don't ask!"

Carter kept quiet.

They pulled away and drove into town, turning right at the main drag and then into the large NAAFI complex. The NAAFI had a major branch in the town, supplying the three regiments with their general groceries and white goods. They turned into the deliveries only road and followed it to the back of the store. Then Barker parked up the car and they both made their way to a delivery door, where Barker asked for Pete. A young man in NAAFI uniform came out and gave them the nod. Carter and Barker were ushered into the loading bay area of the store, and then led to an office.

"How's it going Colin? Thought the Escort was bought and paid for?"

"Got one more week on guard duty before I nip her back to the UK. You got all the gear I ordered?"

Carter was a bit perplexed for a second. 'Gear!' He had heard that term when he was at Sixth Form College.

"Yeah, I have it. Six boxes of tea bags, three cases of Glenfiddich, four cases of HP Sauce and a thousand cigarettes – two hundred of each brand."

"Thanks." Barker handed over an envelope of money, which was carefully counted.

"Who's your mate?"

"Oh, sorry Pete! This Chris Carter, new guy in the regiment."

"Nice to meet you, Chris!" and he nodded to Carter.

"Ok, Pete and Chris, lets load this stuff into the Escort and I'll get out of your hair, Pete."

They loaded the boxes into the boot and back seat of the Escort, and then they got in the car and drove out onto the main drag.

"What's this stuff for then? You having a party?"

"You'll see."

They drove for about ten minutes to the other side of town, and then drew up outside the door of a large hotel. Barker jumped out and spoke to the doorman, who nodded. He got back in the car, turned into a smaller street and then drove along the back of the hotel. A man with a big handlebar moustache was already waiting.

"Ahh, Mister Barker!"

"Hi there, Claude! I have all your stuff."

"Ja, Ja! Gut!"

"Come on Carter, give me a hand!"

They took out a box of tea bags, a selection of the cigarettes and three bottles of Glenfiddich and followed Claude into the back of the hotel. They were then led to a store room where they put the goods on a table. Claude checked them and handed over some money to Barker. "See you again next week, and here is your order!" Then he passed a piece of paper to Barker, who looked at it quickly before putting it in his back pocket. "Thanks, Claude. See you next week!" and the two men got back in the car.

"So that's it! You're selling stuff to hotels."

"Yep! They love English tea bags – can't get decent stuff over here. I sell them to a few hotels, but now I've found someone who buys them bulk. We get the stuff tax free from the NAAFI. I buy in bulk and sell for a profit. A few months ago I got called in by the NAAFI manager about my purchases and had to cut him in on five percent, so I put my prices up."

"Who'd have thought it - tea bags!"

"You ever stayed in a European hotel? Tea is always shit. If we think it's shit, then the locals must. These guys sell my tea as a specialist tea for the locals. I make money, they make money, everyone is happy."

"So the car then, what was that?"

"Another thing over here: we can buy cars tax free. The NAAFI has a quota of cars, so I sell one in the UK before I buy it here. For example, someone wants an XR3i but goes on a waiting list for twelve months: I can get one over here within a month. I get twenty-five percent up front, and order the car here on HP. Then I buy the car, drive it back to the UK, valet it and then pass it on for more than it sells in the UK. One: they get the car they want without waiting; two: I get it fifteen percent cheaper than the book price; three: I sell it for higher than the book price because of the waiting list. Make on average about five K per car. This baby will make me seven K. I'm off back to the UK after guard duty. Fill the car with cigs, booze and the odd porno movie and spend my time in the UK selling the stuff. "Join the army, be the best' – no! Join the army and make a bit of cash."

"I've never seen you about since I've been here. Where do you hide?"

"I don't go out. I read my books and I volunteer for guard duty. Like I told you, most guys will sell me their guard duties. I'm not a soldier - worked that out when I arrived here - just doing my time. I discovered this money making game and I'm concentrating on that. I've been here a just under a year now and I already have thirty K clear in the bank."

"Not bad! Why the HP then on the cars?"

"One thing you need to remember, always look poor. If I was to rock up with cash for a new car every six to eight weeks as a corporal in the Royal Signals, alarm bells would ring and I'd have the MP's on me and God knows what else."

"What do you do with all your money?"

"I send it back to the UK. I have a load in the premium bonds and the rest in a high interest account."

"And why are you showing *me* around?"

"I thought you might like to help me. I'm getting more

customers now than I can handle."

"So, why don't you bottle-neck and keep to your capacity?"

"Not in my nature!"

"But you don't even know me."

"I've been watching you, though. You've been here a while and you still haven't blended. You're in Toz's room, but you haven't joined that freaky gang, and you haven't sided with Jonah either. I could have you moved and you could join me."

"What do you mean you could have me moved?"

"The OC is ok with me. I could speak to him, have you moved into my room. Then we could then set up our own little show."

Carter looked at him: he wasn't sure. This guy seemed a bit freaky, maybe clever but a bit freaky. Was he gay?

"Let me think about it."

"Ok! I've got a few drop offs to do, and then do you fancy lunch?"

***

Carter lay on his bed reading through the last few pages of his Lesley Thomas book. Toz, Lenny and Mark were on the sofa smoking cigarettes and watching some girl being fucked by a group of black men. Did they never get bored with that shit? he thought to himself – and for a bunch of guys that couldn't stand blacks, Asians, or any form of foreigner they seemed to get a strange kick out of watching naked black men. Carter looked at the time on his stereo and saw it was coming up to six. He was going to jump in the shower in a bit and get ready for his guard duty.

"I hear you're stagging on with Barker, Carter!" Toz shouted from the sofa. "Should get on well with names like that. He's a faggot tech too!"

Carter did not know whether to answer or not.

"You getting on with that fag? Just does guard duty to get out of normal work, and then goes out and about in his flash cars. I bet he goes out picking up little boys!" Lenny and Mark laughed. "Sits in his room all night reading books because he's too scared to mix with the lads."

Carter got up and made his way to the shower.

"Go on, fag! Get yourself dolled up for your boy-friend!"

As he walked past Toz Carter was sorely tempted to drive his fist into his ugly face. He felt the heat building in his head and his fist clenching, but managed to walk on by. He knew he could take Toz, but it just wouldn't be worth the hassle of all the inevitable knock-on ef-fects. It would only make his life hell. Later on, when he was leaving, he heard Toz telling Lenny and Mark they should all go out and find some girls. After the film he had seen he was feeling a bit frisky. He smiled wryly to himself: Toz would get turned on by anything shagging anything - weirdo!

Carter and Barker were on the Gate, the sun just set-ting, when a blue Ford Sierra pulled up. Carter walked over to see who it was and check the passes. It was Ingrid. She was leaning over to the glove compartment to get the car pass, and then turned and recognised Carter. She smiled and showed the pass. "Hi, Chris! Not seen you for a while."

Looking down at the pass he could see she was wearing

a short summer dress. "Hi! It's only been a few days. I've been doing guard duties; I'm on guard duty for the next few weeks."

"That's ok. You want to meet up tomorrow afternoon? I can pick you up in Stuckenburge Strasse just up the road about one o'clock."

"Could do. I've nothing else on."

"Ok, see you then!" Ingrid smiled and drove on in- to the barracks. Her car was stopped at the VCP and Carter watched as she got out and leant over to open the bonnet. Why not, he thought to himself; he hadn't had sex for a while. Barker was watching him as his eyes left Ingrid. He made no comment, and nor did Carter, but he could sense Barker's disapproval.

Carter lay on the bed in the back of the guard room. Barker had said nothing more about helping him out with his little buying and selling business, so Carter let it be. It was not really something he wanted to get in- to anyway. Good luck to him, but he *was* a bit of loner and Carter was having enough trouble getting himself settled into this place, without getting involved with Barker. Barker had his own little world and seemed to be able to get on with it. No one seemed to go near him, but then what about that mention of having a word with the OC! Maybe that was it - maybe Barker was a protected man. Carter's thoughts drifted to Ingrid. Staff Green had messed him about, and he felt a pow- erful urge to have some fun now at Green's expense.

A little later on Carter was sitting in the canteen on his own. Barker had skipped breakfast, saying he had things to do, so was off for a shower and would be out for the day. As Carter bit into a sausage, the back of his chair was kicked away. He caught himself before he fell and stood up to see Staff Green's sneering face, which he thrust close to Carter's with an exaggerated sniff. "You stink!"

Carter did not know what to do or say. "You seem to be enjoying guard duty, Carter, so when you finish at the end of next week I must think of something else for you," he sneered. "Toz tells me you're hooked up with the fag Barker." Carter said nothing, his face burning. "You a fag, Carter? You like men's arses?"

Green looked about to see if he had an audience. Toz, Lenny and Mark were a few tables away, smiles all over their faces. A few others Carter recognised were looking away, and Jonah was clearing his plates. Carter said nothing and Staff Green calmly made for the hot plates. He felt like running up behind Green and driving his foot into the back of his knee, but there was nothing he could do about it. He sat back down and finished his breakfast.

***

Carter left the barracks and turned right to walk along to Stuckenburge Strasse. The blue Sierra with Ingrid at the wheel was already there. The windows were down, and she was listening to BFBS Radio. As Carter approached, she smiled and leaned across to open the door. It was obvious that she wore nothing under the loose summer dress, and he could see down over her breasts to the pubic hair between her legs. Getting into the passenger seat, he asked "Where do you fancy going?"

"Don't worry about that - just sit back and enjoy!" replied Ingrid, and she caught hold of his hand and slid it up her skirt. Carter had no intention of holding back: after all he'd put up with from Staff Green, and especially that morning, he was going to enjoy this. He let her place his hand between her legs, feeling her wetness as he slid a finger into her. Ingrid turned to him and smiled. He slid in another finger and then manoeuvred his thumb to her arse, looking at her face to see how she was reacting. Keeping her eye on the road, she opened her legs a bit more to allow him access. When he slid his thumb into her arse she gave a small moan. Carter felt his cock harden.

Twenty minutes later, they pulled up to a hotel entrance. Ingrid was practically sitting on his thumb and he had three fingers in her; she had been rocking gently back and forth while she drove. As soon as she stopped the car she turned and kissed him passionately on the lips. "I want you Carter!"

After checking in they made their way to their room, where Ingrid lost no time in lifting off her dress and making her way to the bed. She sat there with her legs apart and her hands between them. "I want you in my mouth Carter!" she purred. Carter walked to the bed, unzipped his trousers and placed his cock in her mouth. He held the back of head and started to fuck her mouth – and he was not being gentle. All he had in his mind was Green's Face. "Are you a fag, Carter?" He pulled harder on Ingrid's head, driving his cock further into her mouth and throat. She gagged and hit his legs with her hands. Then he pulled out of her mouth and grabbed her by the shoulders, throwing her face down onto the bed. He jumped onto the back of her legs, pulled her arse apart and placed his cock on her arsehole. She was too dry so he moved back slightly, spat on her, then licked his hand and rubbed it on his cock. Feeling for her wet vagina, he rubbed some of her wetness into her arse. Ingrid offered no resistance, just moaned as he opened her up with his fingers. Then he placed his cock on her arsehole and slowly pushed into her, feeling the tension around his cock as Ingrid moaned and pushed her arse back to meet him. He was aware of her muscles relaxing as his whole cock slipped into her, and then he started thrusting. 'You like men's arses, Carter?' The image of Green's face came to him again. 'No, I like your wife's arse, you cunt!' Carter thought as he pounded Ingrid.

A few minutes later he came hard, leaving his cock in while he felt all his seed pulse. Ingrid didn't move: he had felt her muscles contract as she orgasmed just before him.

When at last he pulled himself out of her and walked over to the bathroom to wash his cock, Ingrid turned over and lay there watching him. "That was great, Chris! That was the best shag I've had in years. I love the rough stuff." Carter looked at her: he had done all that out of hatred for another man, and she had loved it.

"Can you do that again? This time can I use a toy as well. I like the feel of both holes filled, I always wonder what it would be like to be fucked in both holes at the same time."

Carter just nodded as she leant over to retrieve something from her bag.

Chapter 11

Carter stood in the troop office. He had done his week of nights and then a week of days, and now his guard duty had finished. During the day duty he had been given constant hassle not only by Staff Green on the Gate, but also by Lieutenant Harrington. Green had made it his mission to make Carter's life a misery, and he was now a target for all the troop staff. He had no idea what was fuelling this victimisation, but the more Staff Green pushed Carter, the more Carter pushed his wife.

During the day guards he had seen Ingrid a couple of times in the evening, and had played around with her fantasies. They had gone out drinking one evening and Carter got into a conversation with a German guy in a bar. Later that night he had dared Ingrid to flirt with the man. Carter and the German guy kept buying her drinks until she was a little drunk, and they had gone back to the man's house. Carter watched Ingrid fuck the man, and afterwards he asked the guy if he had a friend who could join them on another night. When he agreed Carter took his home number and promised to arrange something, and the man had smiled and nodded. Back at the car Ingrid had asked, "Did you like that? I loved it. It turns me on being watched.

My husband is such a prude. Won't do anything to me, says it is not natural; won't even lick me."

Carter just nodded. "I liked it and so did he."

"So why did you not join in? I wanted you to join in."

"I was tired and I just wanted to see what you would do."

Ingrid was too pissed to drive really but Carter didn't care. If she got nicked for drinking and driving that was her lookout, and something that Staff Green would have to deal with.

"What can I get you doing, Carter?" Staff Green was sitting behind his desk tapping a pen on the note pad in front of him. "I know! You can sweep the garages."

'For fuck's sake!' Carter thought to himself. I spent twelve months doing technical training, learning about how all these army communications systems work, and I all I've done since I got here is earth lugs, guard and now sweeping. Fuck it!'

"Get a broom from the store - I will inspect at three pm!"

He knew what to expect when three pm came, and he wasn't disappointed. By the time Staff Green had finished, the garage was in a worst state then when Carter started, and for not completing the sweeping properly he was put on Restriction of Privileges (ROP's). He had been told to parade in Number Two dress at the Guard Room at seven pm. Green was Duty Sergeant and spent the night giving Carter a hard time. This went on week after week, just getting worse. Carter did nothing wrong, but Staff Green ridiculed him at every step.

Meanwhile, Carter got bored with pushing the boundaries with Ingrid: she *had* no boundaries. He arranged for the German guy they'd met to bring a friend round to his house, and when Ingrid saw there were two men awaiting her she was more than happy to entertain both of them. Carter came in her mouth as the two Germans took turns fucking both her holes at the same time. Carter was finding her more and more tiresome. It was impossible to get rid of his frustration on Green's wife because she positively enjoyed everything he did to defile her.

Carter still kept himself at the front of the squad on their runs, determined to sustain a high level of fitness. He relished outdoing Staff Green on the BFT and any of the runs, which quite obviously frustrated the older man. Something in Carter's brain was telling him it would be wiser to let Green beat him, but he was not listening.

It was the troop range day, and Carter had been appointed to look after the butts. This meant being at the end of the range and ensuring the targets were scored up correctly and also patched up with paper and glue ready for the next shoot - Figure 11 targets looked like a soldier running towards you with a rifle. With the SLR a regular soldier was trained to shoot up to 600 metres distance.

The sun was up and the smell of cordite was somehow very comforting. The targets were raised by a pulley and you heard the order to shoot. This was followed by a fizz in the air and a crack as the rounds hit the targets. The targets were then lowered and the scores given. You had to get over 65 for a pass, and if you got over 90 you scored Marksman. Today, when the soldiers on each butt tallied the scores, one of the targets scored the shooter less than 65 and Carter shook his head. If a shooter failed to score 65, they had to shoot again. This could go on all day and make it a late return to barracks. Once back at barracks you had to clean your weapon and today was Friday. Carter wanted to get out into town tonight. He had a date with Lemska later.

Now, though, everyone was achieving above the required score. Carter sat at the end of the row of butts next to the field telephone, watching the soldiers with the targets patching them, raising them; lowering them, patching them. The soldiers in the butts had all done their shoot first thing this morning. The next group to shoot were lined up. Carter got the list from the field phone, smiling grimly when he discovered that Staff Green, Sergeant Bickerstaff, Toz, Lenny, Mark and Jonah were up next. Shooting started, and the butts were lowered, scored, patched, raised until the shoot finished. The field telephone rang. Carter picked it up and was asked for the scores: Green 50; Bickerstaff 65; Toz 45; Lenny 40; Mark 65 and Jonah 94. Hardly had these been called out over the range tannoy than Carter heard the voice of Staff Green cursing and swearing. Within minutes Green had jumped into the butts pit and stormed up to Carter, grabbing him by the front of his combat jacket. "You think that's fucking funny, you cunt?" he snarled. "You think it's funny to make *me* look like a cunt?" He pushed Carter violently back into the bench, sending the tea bouser flying.

"Next time score me correctly, or I'll fucking have you Carter!" And he stormed off out of the pit.

Carter looked along the butts and all eyes were on him. Some heads were shaking; others turned away when he looked at them.

'Probably not the cleverest thing to have done!' he thought to himself. Then the shooting started again, with Carter sending the scores back to the range marshal.

Barker came up to Carter as the squadron was packing away. "What did I say about you keeping your head down?"

"What are you talking about?"

"You and Staff Green. I know he doesn't like you, but why pull a stunt like that! No one thought it was funny. Have you got a personal self-destruct button?"

"No! I'm just sick and tired of him fucking picking on me."

"So you think it's a good idea to make him look like a cunt in front of his men doing what he's renowned for being good at! He wears the cross rifles of a weapons' instructor for fuck's sake. He leads the Bisley shooting team for the Regiment."

"I didn't think it through." Carter lowered his head.

"Well you need to get a grip before something bad happens. This is the Army, and some bad shit has happened here in the past. People have been hurt and some have gone fucking missing. AWOL is the report, but normally if you go AWOL it means you've run home. Some people, though, have never been heard of again."

Carter looked into Barker's eyes.

"You *are* joking?"

"Don't be a cunt, Chris! Remember where you are! No one gives a fuck about us. We're soldiers in a foreign country and we follow our own rules. Do you think Staff Green would get away with this shit if this was a factory back at home?" Carter looked about him: watched everyone packing up the range, doing their tasks, cleaning weapons, taking tables and tents down, loading wagons – all going like a well-oiled machine. "Think about it, Chris, and don't fight it! You need to fit in, or you're an outsider. You've no choice but to submit to Green and his cronies – to become part of this machine."

Barker moved away and Carter's stomach felt weak. Next to walk over was Jonah. "Now that was fucking funny! You should have seen Staff Green's face. He was fucking fuming. I laughed my fucking socks off. They were all clustered around cursing you. If I were you, I'd be out of barracks as soon as we get back. They'll be after your blood, and Staff Green has proper stirred them up."

"You fancy going out tonight? I'm meeting up with Lemska at the Go-Park."

"I'll meet you down there, but I can't be seen with you at the moment. You're not a popular guy!"

"Too hot to be with at the mo!"

"I have to think of my own reputation, Chris. You're a nice guy, but you've picked a fight with the wrong person."

"Picked a fight? I didn't pick a fight! That fucking tosser Micky set this up before I even got here!"

"But you didn't have to prove his point. You could have blended in and all this would have gone away. All you've done is feed the fire."

Carter looked at Jonah. "I didn't stand a chance."

"Yes, you did! You could have slapped Toz. You could have fucked one of the girls in your room with the guys, but all you did was play high and mighty with them."

"You said yourself they were tossers."

"So they are, but that doesn't stop you having a drink with them. You could've played along with Toz. Nothing to stop you having a bundle with him - he would have respected you for it; then you should have had a party with one of the birds they get hold of. Toz loves nothing more than ganging some poor pissed bird. Never seems to have one on his own, ganging seems to be his thing."

"So I slap him now! Fuck a slut with him."

"Too late, gone too far; they think you're an arrogant twat and won't let you in now"

"Fuck! I hate this place."

"The best thing is try and get a transfer. Volunteer for a specialist unit, like 264, 216, 13 Intelligence, the Marines. We've got a squadron based in Plymouth. You're fit enough. Just try to get the fuck out of here!" Jonah turned and made his way over to help a group of soldiers loading a truck with ammo cases. Carter made up his mind that was what he'd do on Monday – volunteer the fuck out of this regiment.

***

Sergeant Bickerstaff's Land Rover – one of the new V8 petrol vehicles - was carrying some of the unused ammo back to barracks, and Carter asked if he could drive. He wanted to be first back to barracks, so once behind the wheel, he really gunned it. "That was a funny stunt, Carter," laughed Bickerstaff. "Not bright, but funny! Green's face was a picture. He's never failed to score the highest on every Range Day. Loves his rifle like a child; spends his time when he's on Duty Sergeant cleaning and checking it." Bickerstaff smiled. "Well, he's certainly going to make your life hell next week! Get your foot down, and I'll let you get away before the rest get back."

"Cheers, Sarge!" Carter smiled, and then added, "I really want out of here. How do I volunteer for one of the specialist units?"

"Come and see me on Monday and I'll have your application submitted. What you planning to volunteer for?"

"All of them - whichever comes up first!"

"SAS are always after techs. Selection's a bit tough, though."

"Has to be better than this place!"

"OK, speak to me first thing on Monday and I'll make sure the applications get approved."

"Cheers Sarge!"

"But you promise me you'll settle down when you move; otherwise you'll be RTU'd straight back here and your life won't be worth living."

"I will, Sarge."

Chapter 12

Carter was standing at the bar of one of the dance floors in the Go-Parc. He looked at his watch: Lemska was due at nine and it was still only eight. He had not seen any of the lads about, so they were probably still in the 'Pigs' Bar' getting pissed on the cheap beer. Most did not head out to town until after eleven when the bar closed. Why pay more than thirty pence a pint! He was on his second drink when Jonah appeared beside him.

"*Here* you are!" Jonah smiled. "Staff Green was doing his nut looking for you - he wanted your bollocks. I think you were going to be on guard tonight."

"Bickerstaff let me go as soon as we unloaded. I grabbed a quick shower and got the fuck out of there. I knew I had about thirty minutes over the Four-Tonner. You guys pulled in just as I was about a hundred yards up the road in civvies. It was close!"

"Your life's going to be hell on Monday. Enjoy yourself while you can!"

"I am putting in for a transfer Monday, and Bickerstaff is going to help me."

"Nice bloke Bickerstaff, but bear in mind your applications are going to take up to two or three months."

"Fuck it! Let's not think about it. Do you want a beer?"

"Is the Pope Catholic!"

At just after nine Lemska found Carter in the pre-arranged meeting place at the bar of the general dance floor. He hadn't seen her for a week and she looked a picture. He kissed her on both cheeks when she came up, and so did Jonah.

"Fancy a drink?"

"Yes please," and as he turned she whispered into his ear. "Missed you, Chris!" He smiled and kissed her on the cheek again. A little later, after sipping some of her drink Lemska asked. "Shall we dance?"

They did; all three of them, Carter, Jonah and Lemska. At around midnight Lemska leaned close to Carter, "I need to go now. Can we meet tomorrow? I would like to see you tomorrow evening on your own."

He smiled. "Sure! Pick me up at the barracks whenever you like."

"Shall we say seven?"

"OK."

"I must go now. Could you walk me to my car?"

"Of course!"

As they went outside, he breathed in the cold, fresh, night air - a welcome relief from the cigarette smoke inside the club. "I really missed you this week, Chris. I did not think I would." Carter smiled and held her hand, pulling her close to him and kissing her on the cheek again. She stopped, turned to him, and kissed him on the lips. "I look forward to tomorrow!" Carter walked her to the multi-story car park and she led him to her car. "I will pick you up at seven tomorrow evening, Chris, sweet dreams!" She started the car, pulled out of the parking space and waved him good bye. Carter smiled, he liked Lemska; she was a nice girl. She was *normal*, and he was looking forward to tomorrow night.

He got back to the bar where he had left Jonah to find that he'd been joined by Ingrid and Suzie. Carter walked up to them. He no longer wanted anything to do with Ingrid, and now he had his way out: he was going to transfer and get the fuck out of this place. Ingrid was a bit drunk and came up to Carter and licked his ear. "I want to feel your cock in my arse tonight, Chris," she slurred. "I want to feel you cum in my arse. I am *really* horny!"

Carter turned and looked at her. This was not what he wanted: from Lemska to this! He saw that Jonah was already all over Suzie.

"Do you want to dance, Chris?"

"No, just a drink. I'll be going soon."

"Well, let's have a drink and you can walk me back to my car."

"Are you fit to drive?"

"Of course I am," Ingrid smiled. "If I get pulled I'll just negotiate with these friendly coppers over here. Wouldn't be the first time!"

"Does your husband know you're like this?"

"What? No, thought I was a virgin when we met. Knows fuck all about what I do, or what I like. Unlike you, Chris! You know that German bloke you set me up with? I had a party with him and his friends the other night. That's right Chris, friends! Six in total. One was black - and God, was he black! His cock was like a baby's arm. I thought he was going to split my arse." She smiled, "Makes me fucking horny just thinking about it."

Carter just looked at her: she was horrible. What had he done?

"Are you walking me to my car? I want to go to my car."

***

Mark was in the back seat of a Mercedes. The woman with him was about forty. She was sucking his cock and he could feel her hard nipples rubbing against his thigh. He had met her about an hour ago, queuing to get a burger. She had helped him order the burger because the young guy behind the counter did not speak English and was struggling with Mark's pointing. She had asked what he wanted, ordered it for him, and then invited him to join her at one of the plastic tables. Her English was ok, if a little broken. After they'd eaten their burgers she asked him to walk her to her car, and once there, had kissed him and ushered him into the back seat. Mark had been on her like a rash, which she seemed to enjoy. One hand now held her head on his cock while he drove three fingers into her arse. She moaned some protest, but he kept a tight grip on her and prepared to cum down her throat, whether she wanted it or not. Then just as he was about to cum he saw Carter walk past the front of the car, with Staff Green's wife. He let go of the woman's head and pulled his fingers out of her. She carried on sucking his cock and tried to grab his hand to go back to her arse, but Mark was watching Carter through the front window, a broad smile on his face.

***

Ingrid pressed the central locking button on her key, then moved to the back seat of the car and sat down, spreading her legs. "I want to suck your cock, Chris!" Carter looked at her for a moment. 'What the fuck!' he thought, 'this'll be the last time' and he undid his fly and let her get his cock out. She stroked it and licked it; then took it in her mouth, holding his balls. After a few minutes he said. "I want your arse. Turn around!"

"Oh yes! Please fuck my arse hard in a car park!"

Chris turned her round; she rubbed her wetness into her arse and he held her by the hips and fucked her. She slapped against his thighs, and he could feel his balls slapping her vagina. He pushed in hard and she squealed. She was liking it. Carter could feel himself about to cum. "Turn around!"

Ingrid turned, and he pushed his cock into her mouth and came. Ingrid sucked his cock clean of cum.

***

Meanwhile, Mark had lost his hard-on. He just could not believe what he had just witnessed. 'Fucking hell!' he thought, Carter had just fucked Staff Green's wife in the arse and then got her to lick his cock clean! Toz was going to love this. The woman next to him was moaning about him going soft. "Give me a minute, Love," he told her. She still held his limp penis in her mouth. Mark watched Ingrid pulled away in her car and then watched Carter walk off. Mark had not been seen.

He turned to the woman next to him. "Fancy a party?"

Chapter 13

Ingrid sat at home watching Rainbow on BFBS TV with Matthew. Boring as it was for her, Matthew loved it. "Which window? The *SQUARE* Window!!" Al was out for his run. He had been gone for an hour, and was due back any time; Ingrid had sorted out some chicken to have in sandwiches for lunch. She heard the gate go. He was home. She knew he'd be sweaty and expected him to go straight upstairs for a bath as usual. Suddenly, though, he was in the living room and looking down at her on the sofa, his eyes wide and red. Next thing she knew, she felt her face explode; then again and again, and she could hear Matthew crying in the back ground. She felt a foot in the ribs, and then between the legs. The world went black.

Staff Green looked down on his unconscious wife, blood trickling from her nose, ears and mouth. He picked up Mathew and took him out of the house. Doreen a few doors down would look after him.

***

Sometime later Ingrid picked herself up from the floor. Matthew was nowhere in sight, but Al Green sat looking at her with a beer in his hand. Her face was a mass of pain and her whole body hurt. "I KNOW!" Green snarled. "You Slag!"

Chapter 14

With his stereo playing Gary Newman's Replica album, Carter was getting ready to meet Lemska. It was six o'clock, and Toz, Mark and Lenny were already out. They had money to burn, as it was the beginning of the month and they'd just been paid. God knows where they found that woman last night! She must have been well into her forties, but they had really been on it with her. At least he only had maybe another eight or twelve weeks of this left. He was just finishing off his look and putting on his aftershave when the door suddenly burst open. It was Staff Green. Carter felt a surge of fear, as he could see that Green was drunk and had a face of thunder. He walked straight up to Carter and grabbed him round the throat. "I fucking *KNOW*, you cunt!"

Carter pushed his arms up to get Green's hands away from his throat. "Know fucking what?"

"Know you fucked my wife!"

Carter laughed. "Me and half a dozen other guys, you limp dick!" he sneered. Somewhere in his mind he'd always known it would get out some time - just hoped he would be away from here before it did.

"What did you say?" Green slapped Carter around the face.

"I *said*, me and half a dozen other guys. She fucking loves it!" and he smiled. "She's even had a black cock up her arse, you knob!" Green punched Carter in the nose, smashing the bone, and he fell to the floor and pulled himself into the foetal position. "Yeah, you cock! I've been fucking her, *and* I've been whoring her out to some of the locals."

Green kicked him in the side. "She's my wife! She's the mother of my son!"

"She's a dirty fucking whore who can't get enough cock," Carter groaned. "Know what? She takes it all ways at the same time. You don't fuck her the way she wants it, so others have to do it for you."

Green kicked him again. "Now every fucker's going to know - your wife likes black cock up her arse!

Green knelt down and smashed Carter's head against the floor. "Not if no one fucking tells them!"

"I ain't the first, you cock! She ain't no Mary Poppins."

Green flew into an even worse rage and started pummelling Carter. When he finally ran out of breath, Carter just about managed to say, "What you going to do about it? This'll get me out of here. That's all I want. You beat me up, and I'll be posted. They won't keep me here after this, you limp dick! Go on, do it!"

Looking round the room, Green noticed a bottle of vodka on Toz's shelf. "Not if you're a suicide." With that, he went and got the bottle and brought it over to where Carter lay helpless on the floor. Then he held him by the neck and poured the vodka down his throat.

"You cunt, someone will see you!" Carter moaned, trying not to drink.

"No they fucking won't! They're all down the bar - it was pay day Friday. Drink, you fucker!"

After emptying the bottle down Carter's throat, Green picked him up and dragged him out of his room to the urinals. He propped Carter up against the wall by the sash window and then opened it wide. Carter was very dizzy, whether from the alcohol or the beating, but he could feel himself being picked up. Green hauled him onto the window ledge and gave him a hefty push.

He watched Carter fall the three stories and hit the ground. Then he smiled, and walked away.

Chapter 15

Carter awoke to a continuous beeping: the beeps were just a second apart and would not stop. It wasn't his alarm clock- or at least not one he was used to. Had one of the lads bought a new clock?

He opened his eyes to a bright, searing light above his bed; he was looking straight into a long fluorescent light. He turned his head to see that he was in a bed with raised bars around it, as if to stop him falling out. Shit! What the fuck was this? Was he dreaming? He looked down the bed and saw that he was wrapped in a blue blanket. As his eyes got more accustomed to his surroundings he realised that he was in a hospital room. 'What the....!'

"Nice to see you've joined the land of the living!" came a voice from the just opened door. Standing there was a nurse in a grey uniform with a red shoulder collar. She had dark hair, but apart from that all Carter could focus on was the smile. "We didn't expect you to pull through." Coming over to the bed, she asked him to open his mouth and promptly inserted a glass thermometer. After a while she removed it, checked it and wrote something on a pad.

"How are you feeling, Soldier?"

"Where am I? What's happened?"

"You're in a military hospital, and you've have had a serious accident."

"Accident! What accident?"

"Settle down again for now and a doctor will come in later and talk to you. Would you like some water?"

Suddenly Carter realised he was thirsty. "Yes – please!"

The nurse walked over to his bed, poured a glass of water and passed it to him. When he tried to sit up, though, he was stopped by a terrible stabbing pain that spiked from his neck and shoulders.

"Stay where you are. You've had some serious injuries."

She brought the glass to Carter's lips for him to drink.

"Just lie there and let me help you."

"But what happened to me?"

"As I said, a doctor will be in later to talk to you"

With this the nurse left the room.

***

"Corporal Carter, or can I call you Chris?" The Army doctor stood by his bed.

"Chris is fine."

"Well Chris, you've sustained some serious injuries. You have fractured your spine, damaged a bone in the wrist and have a fractured skull just above the right eye."

"What! How the hell did all that happen?"

"You don't remember?"

"No!"

"You were found on the floor outside the back of your accommodation block. It looks like you fell three storeys. You have been here a month now, and you're lucky to be alive, my lad," the doctor said in a matter of fact manner. "I am a specialist in bone injuries."

"A *month*!"

"Yes - a month, and in and out of consciousness the whole time. I am fairly confident that the fracture to your back is stable, though, and that if we just let it rest and heal itself you will be fine. It will never be a hundred percent, but near enough." He smiled at Carter. "You are an exceptionally lucky young man. As well as the back injury, your stomach is heavily bruised and your organs took some shock from the fall. After all, you fell about forty feet! You have had a catheter fitted but once your bruising has relaxed and the swelling to your spine has reduced, you will function as normal." He paused before adding, "you took a heavy knock to the skull, cracking it above the right eye. You also had some swelling on the brain, but fortunately the crack in the skull and the gash to your face released the pressure from the brain, otherwise it would have been a lot worse.

I can only repeat, you are a very lucky young man! An injury like that could have resulted in permanent brain damage. The one thing that we don't understand is how you managed to break three ribs. Those injuries just do not tie in with a fall."

***

Carter had seen doctor after doctor for the last few weeks. He had been very sore, but had slept through most of it with the aid of the pain killers they were giving him. Now he was starting to get back to normal. His back hurt like hell and he still could not move his legs properly, but they said it was only a matter of time. His back was swollen and apparently this affected the spinal nerve, or something like that. He had seen his face in a mirror a few weeks ago and had been shocked by what he saw. There was a massive lump above his right eye, with a four inch tear in his skin. Jesus! What the fuck happened? He still had absolutely no recollection of any events of that day. All he knew was that he had been found on the swimming pool side of his block by the patrolling guard.

A butch- looking nurse walked into Carter's room, with an expression of some distaste. 'Right! It's time to get rid of this now." She pulled his sheets back and undid the catheter from its bag. "Relax! This is going to feel a bit strange." As she slowly pulled the catheter from his penis it felt as if it was coming from the core of his pelvis. Shit, that was a weird sensation! - a mixture of pain and feeling like you were cuming. When he looked at the catheter he was glad he hadn't been conscious when they fitted it, as it was a lot bigger than his Jap's eye of his penis.

Two nurses came in to soap his body. He was still unable to wash himself; still more or less paralysed from the chest down. They came into his room every morning and evening and ran a sharp object across the sole of his foot for reaction, but there was still very little feeling. It had been three months since the accident, but the doctor said it was still too early to worry - he would be fit as fiddle before he knew it. The two nurses giving him sponge baths were both young, in their early twenties. One was pretty, the other a bit butch for his liking.

"Look at this, Cathy!" one nurse said to the other. "No feeling whatsoever." Cathy laughed.

"Look, I'm wanking it and it's not doing anything... shame!" and both girls giggled.

Carter looked at the ceiling. He didn't know whether to laugh with them or cry. Two pretty girls playing with his cock and he had no feeling in it!

***

"I am detective Spencer and this is Sergeant Hall. We are from SIB - Special Investigation Branch. We are part of the Royal Military Police and have been asked by the hospital to talk to you about your injuries and how you received them."

Carter looked at the two figures towering over his bed. Spencer was a bald, stocky man of about five feet ten, and Sergeant Hall was a woman in her late twenties with blonde bobbed hair, which made her look tomboyish.

"As I keep telling the doctors, I can't remember anything except waking up in hospital."

"The reason we're here is that the doctors reported three broken ribs and bruising, and that indicates a beating. Were you beaten up in the week before the incident?"

"As I said, I can't remember. I don't think so."

"Ok, is it *possible* that you were beaten up prior to the incident?"

Spencer kept asking the questions, and Hall was writing in a note book.

"I just don't know!"

"I hear you're not a popular lad in your unit; didn't really fit in. Liked to joke about, piss around."

Carter looked at Spencer and thought, fucking hell, here we go again!

"Do you know that Staff Green was arrested for beating up his wife on the same day that your incident occurred?"

"No!"

"Could this be a coincidence? Did you know Staff Green's wife?"

"Seen her about."

"Staff Green didn't like you, did he?"

"Not really!"

"Were you sleeping with his wife?"

"No."

"Rumour has it you were."

"No!"

"Ok, we'll let you rest now, but we'll be back tomorrow. Think about what has happened to you, and try and remember the events that led you to being here."

"What's happened to Staff Green?"

"Nothing! His wife has gone back to the UK with the child, and no charges were pressed against him. Domestic: nothing we could really do but give him a slap in the cells for hitting a woman. He's now living in the Sergeants' Mess."

***

Jimmy and his wife Suzy sat next to Carter's bed. Carter had no idea why Jimmy, a skinny little man, was there; he'd only spoken to him a few times, on guard duty. Jimmy was a combat signaller, which was a general run- around job within the Royal Signals. They acted as clerks, helped out in the guard room, and got given tasks as 'RPs'- Regimental Police. The two of them had been visiting Carter every other day for over a week now. He relayed some messages from Jonah and Barker, and he seemed to like visiting – maybe because it got him out of the barracks for half a day at a time.

Suzy was a strange one! She had a very squeaky voice and the largest breasts Carter had ever seen, combined with a very slim body. When Jimmy first visited he brought a carrier bag with six beers, some porno mags and two hundred cigarettes. The nurses had confiscated the beers and the mags.

Jimmy smiled as he sat there, talking of just about anything. He would arrive at two, and leave at half four. Under her coat his wife always wore ultra-revealing tops. As soon as she came into the room she would remove her coat and then lean over Carter as she got him water, or helped him eat something. Jimmy just seemed to sit back and enjoy the show. He had stopped with the porno mags after a telling off from the head nurse, and now seemed to be offering his wife as a substitute.

"I hear you've got some feeling coming back in your feet Chris?" said Jimmy one day.

"Yes, they hurt me with the sharp run they do on my feet. They'd been so used to me not feeling anything, and I yelped"

"That's good!"

"It may not take long now to get up out of this bed."

"You been watching the Formula One?"

"Yes, another good season."

"Looks like Senna will get the championship"

"Mansell's doing well, though. I reckon he may get it this year."

"Do you fancy anything to drink, Chris?"

Carter was feeling a little guilty. He couldn't help liking the way Suzy leant over to give him a drink, revealing a full view of her breasts. He was sure she was getting more flirtatious the more often she did it. He even dreamt about her not wearing a bra, of seeing her large breasts in the flesh. He felt really guilty because Jimmy had been such good company. He had brought him loads of books, and even a Walkman and some tapes to play on it.

"I think I can manage it myself, Jimmy."

"Let Suzy help you, she likes to help you. She feels sorry for you being cooped up in here." Jimmy smiled. "Shit! I nearly forgot. Would you like to see some pics from our holiday last summer?"

Suzy came over to the bed, filled a glass on the side cabinet, then leant over and put it to Carter's lips. Carter looked into her eyes, she smiled at him and he couldn't help but look down. He felt his cock harden. Shit! It wasn't a full hard- on, but at least he felt some movement in it.

***

Carter lay in his bed, still in a single room. They had said they did not want to move him until the injury to his head had settled down. It was slightly infected and the cut was having trouble healing. He didn't mind having a single room; it gave him time to read. He had worked his way through Lesley Thomas, Tom Sharpe and as many Destroyer books as he could get his hands on. The Walkman Jimmy had given him, which had a tape player and a radio function, had been a godsend. Thinking of Jimmy, Carter smiled; he was such a skinny little man with a pencil moustache. He looked no older than eighteen, though in fact he was in his late twenties. Then there was his wife, with her high-pitched voice and a face that was not far from simple. It had been weird looking at Jimmy's holiday snaps. 'Here is a picture of us by a church in Greece; here's Suzy topless on the beach; here we are riding camels; here is Suzy topless on our balcony,' and on it went. Carter could never remember seeing anyone with such large breasts, and Jimmy obviously liked showing them off.

He settled back with his book. The nurse would be round in another half an hour with tablets for the night.

***

Carter was now moving his legs, but was unable to bend them at the knee. He could swing off the bed, though, and could get himself into a wheel chair. He was taken to physio daily and practiced walking along the bars. He was getting better at moving, a lot better in the pool and could feel himself getting stronger. His head hadn't healed as well as they had expected, and one of his eyelids had become lazy. They said it was nerve damage and would get better, but the left eyelid still wouldn't fully open. The scar tissue had swollen in under the skin, due to the infection and the bone healing. He now had a ridge from the corner of his left eye to the top of his hair line. If he touched it, it hurt. He didn't really notice his eyelid unless he looked in the mirror, and when he did he just hoped the swelling would go down, as it did make him look deformed and ugly.

***

Jimmy and his wife came daily and now Carter believed it was a game of how much flesh Suzy could show him. The bra had gone, the skirts had got higher; it seemed like a game they liked to play together, Jimmy always smiling at his wife. God knows what they would do when Carter got moved into a four-man room, but meanwhile it was fun entertainment. Jimmy brought in the papers, and Carter liked to chat to him about Formula One. Also Jimmy now had it as a mission to find the books Carter liked. He kept turning up with James Herbert, Jack Higgins, and even some erotic fiction. The last got raised eyebrows from the some of the nurses, and Carter was sure a few had gone missing during the night as he slept.

Jonah and Barker had come in a couple of times, had a laugh and a joke and then gone again. Carter was happier now that he was getting better, and he liked the simplicity of Jimmy's company.

***

It had been six months, and at long last Carter was reasonably able-bodied and was moved into a four- man room. One of the others was Hodgson, a young corporal who'd had his left knee shattered in a skiing accident. He was with the Royal Green Jackets, and just before the accident had passed Senior Brecon at the age of only twenty-four: his career was now over. Simpson had lost most of the skin on his hand in Norway. As part of his night duty he had been filling up a paraffin heater, spilled some on his hand without realising, then re-gloved and gone back to sleep in his snow hole. In the morning the hand had been frozen like an icicle, the fingers were practically stripped to the bone, but he was lucky to still have any hand at all. Then there was Rogers, the piss-head of the room. He had been stabbed with a hunting knife, arguing with his friend when they were both drunk about who had the sharpest knife. His mate showed him how sharp his knife was by stabbing him in the chest, puncturing a lung.

Rogers was a character, though! When he was in isolation in intensive care and on a breathing machine he would hold his breath until the alarms went off. When the nurses came rushing in he would breathe again, and then ask for a cup of tea while they were there. His wife got banned from bringing him oranges because she used a hypodermic to inject them with vodka. It took three nights for the nurses to work out how he managed to get paralytic every night. When he saw Suzy on the days she and Jimmy came to visit all they heard was, 'Look at the knockers on that! Fuck me!' which made Jimmy smile and Suzy go red. After a few days on the mixed ward Jimmy was bringing in papers for all the lads and Suzy was keeping everyone's end up, while Carter shared his books with the room. When the head nurse came around at ten for lights out she would ask how everyone was. The responses were always the same: 'feeling a bit spunky;' 'got a bit of swelling that needs attention," and so on, and every night Rogers would go on and on about Suzy.

"Aren't you married Tom?" Carter asked.

"Yeah, I am - but what she don't know don't hurt her!" Rogers laughed. "Only looking! Maybe touching, and biting if I had the chance, and wanking all over them if my dreams could come true."

"And what would you do if your missus was all over some black guy now?"

"I'd fucking kill her, the slag!"

"Well, it'd only be the same as what you're thinking of doing."

"*Not* the same, though. It's different for guys. We ain't slags"

The response to this statement was a roomful of debate for the next hour.

Later on. "Anyway, I'd love those tits in may face. Would love it!"

"Well, why don't you ask her!" the room said in unison.

As the weeks passed, Rogers kept talking about Suzy, but never asked her to indulge his fantasy. Carter believed that if he *did* ask it would probably happen, but he wasn't going to tell him that! Suzy had taken to wearing t-shirts with no bra, which left nothing to the imagination, and the boys loved it. Rogers and Hodgson's wives didn't look too happy at the sight, but Suzy cheerfully ignored them.

***

"We are going to let you out for a holiday, Carter," the head doctor said one day. "You have been here six months now; you seem to be walking properly and your back is stable. I'm sorry about the eye and the lump on your head, but there seems to be nothing we can do about it."

"Thank you, Sir!"

"I will have a chit signed with a leave pass and some travel warrants. I suggest you have a three week break back home with Mum and Dad."

Chapter 16

It felt strange getting off the train at the end of the branch line. Carter had been lucky the tube had been running ok and he had managed to get the Central Line to Debden, and because the rush hour hadn't yet started had easily managed to get himself a seat. His mother's house was just down the road from the station, so he managed to carry his bag without too much discomfort. His back did not hurt him that much but his left leg felt a little numb, as if it had gone to sleep. He had been assured this was still down to nerves affected by the injury to his back, and would wear off in the next few months. The doctors were happy with his recovery and had told him he would be back to full fitness in no time.

His mother lived in a row of four old cottages along the side of the railway line; theirs was called Rose Cottage and had a big rose bush rambling round the entrance. The cottage was old, and still had an open fire but a lot of the inside had been modernised, with a fully fitted kitchen and all the mod cons in the living room. As soon as he walked through the unlocked door, his mother called out. "Is that you, Chris?"

After numerous cups of tea, some slices of cake and his mother moaning about why he had joined the army and that no good would come of it, Carter had made his way out of the house and had gone for a walk into Debden. He had called Amanda's home from the house phone and had been told she was working at weekends in the local fish and chip shop. She worked there at weekends as a waitress and during the University Holidays.

He had been seeing Amanda as a girlfriend from the age of sixteen. She was a few months younger than him and born in September, which had placed her a year below him in school. They had first met at Sixth Form College, where Carter had been finishing his 'A' levels and she had just started hers. Instead of going to university and studying for a degree, Carter had joined the Army, while Amanda had followed the expected path and enrolled at Hatfield Polytechnic – soon to become Hertfordshire University as part of the plan to keep young people off the dole queue by encouraging them all to do degrees. She was about to start her first year at the Poly later in the month.

Not only had he not seen Amanda for ten months, but he had only written once since arriving in Germany. He felt bad now, realising how he had neglected her, and wondered what she might have to say to him.

The fish and chip shop was both a take-away and a restaurant. The take-away side had a service counter, and the other had chairs and half a dozen wooden tables spread with red and white checked cloths. He saw Amanda immediately, smiling as a couple at one of the tables ordered their meal. He watched her serve, taking in afresh what she looked like, with her shoulder length, light brown hair, slim figure and fresh, smiling face. He stood back from the counter as she came up to the side to place the order. She spotted him, paused for a second, and then carried on with her order. Once it had been dealt with, she looked over and smiled. Carter smiled back.

Carter sat at a table in the Sir Winston Churchhill Pub. It was six o'clock and he was waiting for Amanda to finish work. He had a pint of lager in front of him on the table and was reading Destroyer: Death Check by Warren Murphy. The bar was quiet with only a couple of builders occupying another table.

Amanda came into the bar just after six and asked for a vodka and pineapple juice with ice. They sat chatting for a while until Amanda asked the inevitable question: why had she not heard from him, except for one letter, when she had written seven times? Uncomfortably, Carter explained that he had been on exercise and training and just didn't have time to write, or even call.

What did he expect her to do then? Just wait around for him to get in touch? What was she supposed to do! Carter didn't want this to turn into an argument, so he changed the subject to university. Yes, she was looking forward to going. Then the conversation got round to his accident and injuries. "How did it happen? Is your eye going to heal? It looks a bit nasty!'

They finished their drinks and he ordered some more from the bar.

***

Carter pulled himself off Amanda as she lay on his bed, and rolled onto his back. "I needed that!" she smiled.

He was a bit perturbed; she seemed to have changed a lot in the time he had been away. For one thing, she had been a lot more demanding sexually, and had been the instigator of them going to bed. "Chris," she said now, "there is something I have to tell you. This is going to be the last time we are together." He stayed silent. "When you went away I was sad, and when you never wrote to me, or called me and I never heard from you I got sadder. Then one night when I was out for a walk I met a man with his dog and we got to chatting. He seemed nice, and then he asked me out for a drink, and before I knew it I was in his arms." Carter felt his stomach turn into knots.

"When you met me, I was just a silly little girl who believed that you meet someone, fall in love, get married and live a life like your parents. Well, you've shown me that it isn't like that. You went off on your adventure and forgot about me, and I suddenly found my own adventure. I've slept with several men since you have been away, you know, and it's meant nothing. And what we just did: it means nothing now."

"What!"

"When I saw you again today for the first time in ten months the surprise of it made me happy, but then when I looked at your face and how you have damaged it in your 'adventure', I realised that in all honesty you mean more or less nothing to me now. It makes it easier that you are not the same person; not only your face has changed, but I could tell even when we were talking that *you* have changed. You talk all the time as if you are angry. The gentle, kind boy I knew is now an angry man. My dad warned me it would happen. He said the army is no good, unless you're a certain way."

"So what are you saying?"

"I'm saying, this is it! You can make love to me again if you want but we are finished. I am going to live my life and you are going to live yours."

"What? And who are these men?"

"None of your business. That's all part of *my* life, part of my growing up, not yours."

Carter lay back on the bed, but he couldn't really feel angry. He knew she was right: everything had changed, he had changed.

He did make love to her once more but there was no feeling in it.

***

"You really got fucked up," Smithy laughed over a Castlemaine XXXX. "Look at that fucking eye and that scar! Fuck me!"

Carter and Smithy had been mates since Secondary School. Smithy had gone prematurely bald at eighteen, which had been the subject of much hilarity in their youth, and now Smithy was taking the piss out of Carter. "You ain't going to be pulling the birds looking like that, mate."

"Fuck off, Smithy! Give the injured party a break!"

"As if! You've been taking the piss out of me for my hair for ages."

"How is the bird front Smithy, anything?"

Smithy smiled ruefully. He looked about twenty five but when girls found out he was only nineteen they ran a mile. The other down side was that he hadn't passed his driving test. He was young and bald, and could only hang about the local haunts unless someone gave him a lift.

"Nothing!" Smithy said taking another sip of his beer. "What about you?"

"Well, Amanda dumped me this afternoon."

"No shit there, I've seen her about a few times with various people."

"Yeah well, that's that." They both raised their glasses. "You wouldn't believe the birds you get to mess about with in the Army!" Carter recounted some lurid tales of the girls he had met in Germany, and Smithy was convinced he should join up the following day.

They were both walking home a bit worse for wear after going to The Epping Forest Country Club, the local night spot. "I tell you, Smithy, it's not like here. You don't even have to speak to the girls; they're not a bit up themselves. They'd rather suck your cock than kiss you."

They had both tried to meet girls that night, but with Smithy's looks, Carter's injuries and the amount of alcohol they'd drunk they had got nowhere.

"I am telling you, sex is the norm!" Carter slurred. "Though there is this one girl. She's really nice, but I haven't seen her since the accident."

"What the fuck happened to you anyhow, Chris?"

"I don't fucking know. I just cannot remember. They said I fell out a window."

"Why would you do that?"

"I don't fucking know!"

"Was you pissed?"

"No!"

"So why fall out a fucking window, you cock?

"I *can't* remember!"

"Seems a bit of a strange thing to do."

"The window sills are low, so I suppose I could have slipped."

"Seems odd that you fell out a window though, and you hadn't even been drinking."

For three weeks the same questions from his mother, the same thoughts in his own mind. What *had* happened that night? He knew he'd been getting ready to see Lemska, but he had not met her, nor had he heard from her in all the time he had been in hospital. He did not have her number and she probably didn't know how to get his from the army. Not only that, but he didn't know where she lived either. He had been given three weeks leave. His back didn't hurt as much as he'd thought it would, and he started to go for walks along the disused railway line during the day, trying to jog for some of the way. He was definitely getting better.

He had seen Smithy most evenings. They drank until closing time, but had no luck with any women. Smithy was used to it and it didn't bother him, but Carter was starting to feel self-conscious about the way he looked. He started to let his hair hang over his left eye, but still noticed the curious looks people gave him. It looked like he had an enormous sty, and the scar running to his hair line was still red and angry. Everyone he knew asked him what had happened. The girls he'd known from school and college who used to be a bit flirtatious seemed to be stepping back now. He just did not seem to have the same flair with the girls.

Smithy seemed to be happy just drinking, and commenting on the opposite sex but not doing anything about it. At first Carter was frustrated by this, but as the three weeks rolled by he seemed to get used to it. Eventually the day came for Carter to give his mum a quick hug and pick up his bags. It was time to go back.

Chapter 17

Carter had been discharged from hospital and was standing just outside the barrack gates, wondering what lay in store for him beyond. His back was stable now, and he had been released from the ranks of the sick and deemed fit to return to normal duties.

He had been exceptionally lucky. He had crushed two vertebrae but not seriously, (probably they guessed because his legs had bent when he had landed), and his head had taken a bit of a blow. They still could not understand the broken ribs; the SIB had been back a couple of times and then he had heard nothing. Presumably the only conclusion could be that the body did some strange things.

Picking up his bag he walked up to the soldier at the Gate. His ID was checked, and then he was allowed to enter the barracks. 'That's the guy they found smashed up outside One Squadron block!' he heard from behind him. He did not turn round – just carried on walking. He made his solitary way to the block and upstairs to his room. The lines were empty, as it was ten o'clock in the morning. He opened the door to find everything exactly the same. His bed had been made and the room had not changed in any way. He placed his bag by the bed and went back downstairs to the troop lines. "Get yourself in fucking uniform, Carter!" snarled Staff Green. "What are you doing walking in here in civvies? You're in the fucking Army and you have been discharged from hospital. Get the fuck out of here and get into uniform!"

Carter stood at his locker. He wanted to cry. Slowly he got changed into his green fatigues, pulled on his boots and wrapped the laces around the tops, then tucked his trousers into his elastics. He checked himself in the mirror and then made his way back down to the troop office.

"Ok Carter! I have been told you're now fit as a fiddle, so it's back to the Army time for you. No more soft beds and sexy nurses. So what the fuck am I going to do with you, now you have had a fucking holiday!" Carter looked at Staff Green with silent loathing as he said this. "You can start by going into your workshop and making up some earth lugs. When you ain't got anything more like that to do, I will find something else for you!"

"Yes, Staff."

"Now, off you run, you fucking Biffer."

Carter turned and marched out the office.

Staff Green sat at his desk and smiled. The dopey cunt really didn't know what happened to him on that night! He had sat back and observed from a distance while the investigation had unfolded. Carter had been found on the ground outside the block by the patrolling guard, taken to the Medical Centre and then on to Rinteln Military Hospital. He had a broken back, a smashed up face and some broken ribs. What an ugly fucker he looked now, with that fucked up eye and the scar on his forehead! Green had been told he looked a sight and had lost his pretty boy looks, but hadn't realised quite how much it had changed his face. There had been an SIB investigation and some questions but no one had seen anything, and apart from the broken ribs there was nothing suspicious. It seemed a straightforward case of a pissed soldier trying to get out by suicide.

Green had been angry at the time about Carter and Ingrid, but since she'd gone back to the UK and he had been living in the sergeants' Mess, he had learnt a lot about his wife, and that Carter had not been the first. Green thought he would have been angry about this, but after what he had done to Carter and when his temper had got the better of him, he confronted Ingrid. She had told him everything: about all the men, and about how he did not satisfy her - he just loved his army shit. They said jump, and he did! As he smashed her face she had smiled at him and told him how useless he was and how she had despised him. Told him how she had slept with black men; how she had been shagged by *his* men. At that point he had lost any feeling for her: she was alien to him, and he had smashed her up quite badly. The neighbours had heard Ingrid's screams and called the Military Police, who had arrested and beaten him. Later on they had night sticked him in the cells, and when he fought back he was handcuffed and beaten again harder for hitting a woman.

The charges had been dropped, though, after the Military Police had found out what had happened. At this point he had become the injured party. Ingrid had dropped all charges and gone back the UK with Mathew, and now he'd heard that she had returned to her native Norway. Green couldn't care less; he didn't even miss Matthew. He loved it in the Sergeants' Mess. He was training every day and enjoying beers in the Mess every night. He did not go out down the town. He liked to carry out surprise inspections on the guard and in the troop lines. He was having a ball.

The Regimental Commanding Officer had asked Green to move Carter to Mike Troop, so that the two of them would be separated. Carter could then stay in barracks and fix equipment in the Technical Maintenance Troop. He had disagreed with this and got the backing from the Officer Commanding the Squadron to block the move. He wanted Carter here with him. He wanted Carter to suffer, and he was going to have fun making it happen. He had plans, and he was going to enjoy putting them into action.

Carter made his way up the stairs to his room. It had been his first week back and all he'd been doing was making earth lugs. Then when there were no more to make he was told to sweep the workshop, then to tidy the workshop. Tomorrow he was to stock take, organise everything. He was asked continually about what had happened and he told everyone the same thing. 'I do not know what happened. I can't even remember the day it happened. I just remember waking up in hospital.'

Toz had given him the name Cyclops, said he was as ugly as the 'Sloth' out of 'The Goonies'. They all took the piss out of Carter, especially when he had to sweep and mop the corridor of the troop lines every morning before parade to make up for the time he had been dossing about in a hospital bed.

He had at last had managed to get in touch with Lemska and had met her as soon as possible in the tavern Jonah had taken him to a while ago. She had surprised him by not seeming to find his altered face distasteful. She explained too that she had tried to get in contact with him but no one would tell her anything. Carter had reminded her that he did not have her number and did not know where she lived. Smiling, she said she would take him to her house to meet her parents and show him where she lived, and they had arranged to go this weekend. When Carter got to his room he dropped onto his bed, pulled the pillow over his face and closed his eyes. Shit! What the hell was he doing with his life? At that moment the door opened, and Toz, Lenny and Mark stepped into the room. "Oi Cyclops! What are you doing sleeping?" Toz's voice boomed.

***

Carter was sitting in Barker's room watching Wall Street on video. "I wonder how you get into this game?" Barker asked, more to himself. "This is the third time I've seen this film. I like the idea of this, but how do you get into it?"

"No idea. I think you need a lot of money."

"Shit, I have £38K in the bank now. I am sure that is enough to get started."

Carter took another sip of his beer. Barker had a room of his own and Carter had been spending more and more time in there with him. Barker did not really drink, did not go out. Spent all his time watching films or reading books, and strangely no one bothered him. Toz called him a faggot, but he didn't rise to it, and Toz never pushed it beyond snide comments. It was like Barker and the others had agreed a truce. Barker just seemed to be interested in making his money. His room was full of all the mod cons. His Hi-Fi was top of the range, with Wharfdale speakers linked to his Hi-Fi video recorder and his 32 inch TV. He also had a coffee machine and a desk with a nice light. The walls had some movie posters on them; soon likely, from the way he idolised him, to have a Gordon Gekko added!

"I am definitely looking into this game."

"Looks like something you need to be out of the Army to do."

"I'll resign as soon as my five year point is here. I'll put in my years notice and then one year to go. So in total I have about 3 years left."

"I've got another seven years! I need to get a voluntary posting, or get on to my T1 as soon as possible. I'm fucked spending my time here."

"Why don't you PVR?"

"What do you mean PVR?"

"Premature Voluntary Release, like resigning but you pay to get yourself out."

"How do you do that then?"

"You go to the OC and request it. They can turn you down, though, and if they do you can't apply for another six months. But they can only turn you down three times."

"Got no money - and if they decline it three times, which they probably would, that's eighteen fucking months!

"Go and see the padre and see what he says. He can get you moved. I know someone who went to the padre and he was posted in weeks. Told the padre about his mother being suicidal and all that."

"Why doesn't everyone do that?"

"If he *doesn't* get you moved, your life becomes hell. But you have a good case and your life is hell anyway!" Barker smiled, "What you got to lose?"

"Why do the officers in this unit not do anything about the bullying and bollocks that goes on here?"

"They don't really care. No fucker wants to be here. If you look at the officers here, most are young ones out of training passing through. The seniors are mostly ex-rankers. They're all mad as hatters, and this is what the Army was all about. They lived it and so why change it! Look at the CO, he is ex rank. The Major in your troop lines is ex-rank. The TOT's are all ex-rank as you know. A few others are officers that just do what they are told because they don't want rock the boat. No fucker gives a damn. Look at what happened to you. SIB sniffed about for a day or so and that was that."

"It's wrong."

"It's the Army. Look at what happened here last New Year's Eve. That shooting never hit the news."

"What shooting?"

"You never been told? A corporal and his wife came out of the Corporals' Mess on New Year's Eve after a party. The wife was flirting about with the gate guard, and he let her have his rifle to play with. They cocked the weapon…"

"I thought the weapons on the gate had empty mags on them?"

"Supposed to! The guard had also been on the piss all night. The mags had got mixed up somehow and a live mag was on the rifle."

"Shit!"

"So the wife is holding a cocked, live weapon. The husband sticks his mouth over the barrel of the rifle and asks his wife to pull the trigger. He thinks it's empty and she is only going to fire off the action."

"Shit, no…"

"Yep! Lucky thing was, he turned away from the rifle just as she pulled the trigger. Fired a shot into his upper shoulder…"

"Fuck!"

"Yep, he lost the use of his arm and was discharged from the Army."

"What happened to the guy on the gate?"

"All a big cover up: he went to Colchester nick for six months, and when he came out he was promoted and posted to a cushy number in Cyprus to keep him quiet."

"What, nothing happened here?"

"Nope, the guy on the gate took the wrap on his own; nothing else was said. The corporal was medically discharged and that was that."

"He could have been killed."

"There *have* been deaths here. Suicides, and a couple of lads have gone missing in their time. Whether they are AWOL no one can be so sure."

"I know about the boxer."

"Yeah, there've been a couple of others too. A year or so ago the parents came into the barracks looking for their lad. The Regiment had said he'd gone AWOL but no one had seen him since. He had definitely not gone home."

"Fuck! You wouldn't believe this sort of thing could happen."

"Well, they ain't going to advertise it." Barker looked across to the film. "I am going to be that rich, one day."

"I bet you are!"

***

Lemska's father sat at the head of the table, and Carter was sitting facing her mother, with Lemska next to her. Mother and daughter were quite similar, though the mother looked rather tired around the eyes. She was in her mid-fifties with blues eyes and blonde hair, and Lemska's father was a big, booming sort of man, large in body and large in features, with hands like shovels. His eyes were bright and beaming and he had a beard that filled his face. He had been very friendly and welcoming when Carter had arrived, and was wearing a suit for the occasion. He spoke very good English in a very loud voice. In complete contrast, his wife, whose name was Renate, was like a quiet mouse when she introduced herself.

Lemska's father, Heinrich was sixty five, and from what Carter had gathered was a successful businessman, with interests in civil engineering, construction and property. He blared away at the table, apparently loving the sound of his own voice. Carter smiled at this, but Lemska looked uncomfortable, and her mother just sat quietly, without saying anything. Heinrich had more than enough to say for the both of them. When asked about his face Carter explained that he did not know what had happened, and Heinrich had laughed. As Lemska had already told Carter, he had been stationed in the same barracks In World War Two. Called up in 1943 to serve with the Tank Regiment, he had served on the Russian Front, a bad place to be; had been one of the lucky ones that got out alive. He now held forth about the war. 'They go on and on about the war crimes of the Germans. Does no-one care what the Russians did? Their crimes were worse than any German. Yeah, the Jew thing was bad but six million is chicken feed to what the Russians have slaughtered and are still slaughtering. You want to go to war with them? Rather you than me.'

Lemska interjected to change the subject. "Tell Chris about that new building you are building in Hanover Papa!"

"Ah Ja, I am building a new glass block for a communications company; lots of geld this communications company!" Heinrich boomed. "You do communications, Ja?"

"Yes, I do communications."

"You need to leave army and do communications outside. There is money in communications."

Carter smiled. Lemska's mother stayed quiet.

The impressive meal was served by a staff. Carter had already been astonished when Lemska pulled up in the drive of her parents' house. It was near Lubeck and was a country house that used to be a stud farm. It looked as if it would have everything you that you could ever dream of, and parked outside were a Mercedes SLS and a Rolls Royce. The house was obviously worth a fortune and Carter reckoned that Lemska's parents must be extremely wealthy people. Were worth fortunes. They had a lavish three course meal and drank red wine, followed by an elegant dessert wine with the dessert. After the meal they moved to a large lounge where Heinrich immediately began to pontificate about the forthcoming collapse of Communism and how the fall of the Berlin Wall would cost the West German economy a fortune. The Arabs were going to wreck the world and Hitler *did* have the right idea, just did not execute it properly. Heinrich was a one-way conversationalist, but suddenly, at around midnight he stood up, seemed to gather up Lemska's mother and left the room.

Lemska smiled when the door closed. "He likes you."

"Really? I did not say anything!"

"If he didn't, he would not have left you alone with me now. He would have waited until you left the house before retiring."

Carter smiled and then she kissed him. Carter felt the warmth of her lips on his; he had not kissed properly for so long.

Lemska took Carter's hand and led him to her bedroom.

***

Carter sat in his room thinking about the weekend just gone. He had stayed the Saturday night with Lemska and on the Sunday he had been asked to join the family for a walk. As Lemska had told him, the Germans seemed to love to walk on a Sunday. The family owned two large, impeccably behaved German Shepherd dogs, with Lemska's dad in full control of them. In broad daylight he was even larger than life,

183

and boomed about, laughing and joking about nothing in particular.

They all had lunch in an ale house in the forest on top of Lubeck Ridge. Today Heinrich drank beer, large flagons of beer. Carter could not keep up and did not try to. Lemska and her mother sipped wine. After a few hours in the ale house they made their way home, with Lemska giving Carter a lift back to the barracks. She smiled at him as he got out of the car. "My Papa likes you, Chris. And he does not like many people." 'Could've fooled me!' Carter thought, waving as she drove off. The man was like a big bear!

***

Carter was doing every mundane job in barracks that Staff Green could find him to do. He swept, he mopped, he took the sheets to the laundrette and brought the clean ones back. He issued the bed linen each Wednesday, which was when everyone got a clean sheet and pillow case. He worked in the Sergeants' and Officers' Mess as a silver service waiter when there was a dinner on , and it was Carter who did every Guard Duty if someone did not turn up or reported sick. If Staff Green appeared in his room before seven that meant guard duty, and there was no escape because if he wasn't on guard duty he was on ROPs and had to report to the guard room at seven in his Two dress anyhow.

Green had seen Carter turn up at the front gate one evening with Lemska and the following morning had picked him up for not being smart enough and put him on ROPs; then that evening, as Inspecting Sergeant had given him further restrictions. Carter had not been off Restriction of Privileges for four weeks now, and had no way of leaving barracks. He was not allowed to drink, as he had to parade outside the guard room at seven and eleven p.m in his Number Two dress. His boots were like glass and his uniform spotless, but there was always something. Every Sergeant picked him up on something. Staff Green seemed to have made it a game with all of them.

Carter had just finished his eleven p.m inspection and had been given even extra ROPs for not having all the studs in his boots. One must have fallen out when he walked over to the guard room. Everything else was perfect. His belt buckle shone, his brasses gleamed and his ID was in his top left pocket. Even the church key on his lanyard was in place and shiny (though this was not strictly regulation). Everything! There was nothing more he could possibly have done. He thought he had them beat. Then this: a fucking stud fell out of his boot! As he walked back to block he bumped into Jonah coming out of the Mess with Corporal Watson, from Three Squadron. "Hey, Carter!" Jonah called out. Then "Hey, Carter!" he called again, a bit the worse for wear. Carter went over to them both.

"You got thirty D's on you?"

"Yeah, why?"

"Give it to Mike here, and follow us."

Carter looked at Mike and Jonah.

"Just give it to him, and follow us."

Carter handed the money over to Watson, who smiled as he took it. Jonah slapped Carter on the shoulder. "You're in for a treat!"

Carter followed the two of them into 3 Squadron's

lines, which were the same layout as 1 Squadron's. Mike led them to his room, which like Jonah's and Barker's was a single. It had the usual TV, hi-fi, single bed, sofa and chair. On the sofa was a very pretty girl, slightly inebriated. Mike sat next to the girl who gave him a dozy smile. Mike whispered in her ear and she nodded. Mike got up and left the room, and Jonah sat next to the girl and lifted her top.

Carter just looked at him.

"It's ok. This is Carol. She's Mike's girlfriend and they're both skint. Mike sells her for 30 D's a time so they can have some money to go out." Jonah smiled, he had had a few. "Look at this bod! - and she loves it!" he said, holding one of her breasts while Carol smiled at Carter with glazed eyes.

"She looks out of it!"

"She is, totally. But she loves it. Are you joining in or what?"

"I think I'll pass on this one Jonah," said Carter. "He can have my 30 D's."

"Are you sure? I was thinking we could DP her."

"No thanks. You fill your boots."

Carter turned and walked out of the room. Mike was nowhere to be seen.

***

Jonah joined Carter at breakfast. "You should have stayed last night and had a bit of fun. She's such a fit sort; a body like a model and you can do what you want with her."

"Come on Jonah, she was out of it. That was technically rape."

186

"Is it fuck! Mike does it all the time, gets her pissed and she then earns the money for them."

"It looked like she was more than pissed last night."

"Ah fuck it, Carter! You have too many morals for this place. She didn't scream rape and anyone who sucks your cock until you cum can't be being raped."

"I just didn't feel comfortable with it."

"You're just too loved up with that German bint. How is she?"

"I speak to her on the phone, but I haven't seen her for a month. These ROPs have buggered that up."

"Don't worry about that. We're back on exercise next week for the next eight weeks. Just try and keep out of Green's way."

"Guess so."

***

Staff Green sat in his office and wondered what to do about Carter. He obviously had no recollection of the night he threw him out the window. If he had, he would have squealed by now. He was enjoying messing the boy around. He had a competition on at the Sergeants' Mess to keep Carter in ROPs - who could pick him up for what – but that was getting boring now. Carter did not react to anything; he just seemed to accept his fate and did what he was told. He still wanted to break Carter, wanted to make him run. If Carter went AWOL that would be objective complete. Carter would be busted down to private and end up in the Glasshouse; but Carter seemed to have become a zombie, he rarely went out, kept quiet and just did everything he was told without protest.

Staff Green sat and wondered what to do.

***

Carter, Toz, Lenny and Mark stood by their beds waiting for the arrival of the Troop Officer and Staff Green. The room was immaculate. Everything was cleared away, polished, beds made, floor hoovered and spotless. This was the usual inspection made of the block on a Friday morning, and a main one made prior to going on a long exercise. They could not have the block being untidy while they were away. The ablutions and kitchen were being inspected at the moment, and Jonah was walking around taking any flack if there was anything picked up during the inspection. If the inspection went well the lads would be allowed out for a last blow-out down town before the exercise. If it went badly the troop lines would be re-inspected at 8pm that night.

Staff Green and Lieutenant Harrington walked into the room. They went to each locker and had a look inside, nodded and then ran a finger along the window frames, across the top of the hi-fi and the TV screen. Staff Green opened the fridge, stood for a second and then said, "What the fuck is this?"

Carter was closest to him.

"Come on Carter! What is this?"

Carter turned to look into the open fridge. The fridge was empty.

"This fridge is filthy. Who cleaned the fridge?"

"Carter!!" Lenny said.

"Is that right Carter, you cleaned the fridge?"

Carter nodded.

"It is fucking filthy. Look at the seals, is that mould on the seals?"

Carter looked and could only see some slight discolouration of the seals around the fridge door.

"It is so fucking filthy you could grow mushrooms in that fridge."

Carter said nothing.

"Ok Carter, you were responsible for this fridge. You make sure it is clean and YOU will be here for an inspection at 8pm tonight. These three will not be let down by you and are free to go out tonight."

Toz, Lenny and Mark said thanks to Staff Green and smiled.

Carter sat on the sofa reading the Dark Half, by Stephen King; Toz, Lenny and Mark had headed off down to the bar. The room was spotless and the fridge seals had been bleached. Carter was just waiting for Staff Green to arrive at 8pm. It was five to now.

Carter sat in his green fatigues, he was not going to make that mistake, his boots were shiny and his trousers and shirt were well pressed. There was nothing in his dress that would annoy Staff Green.

At a couple of minutes to 8pm Carter got up and stood by his bed awaiting the appearance of Staff Green, and at 8pm on the dot there he was. He walked into the room, walked directly up to Carter and looked him up and down. Carter could smell alcohol on his breath.

Staff Green looked about the room, seemingly perplexed that it was spotless. He walked over to the hi-fi and TV and ran his finger over them, looking for dust. Nothing! There was nothing he could pick Carter up on in his dress, or in the room.

"Well Carter, let's look at this fridge then." Green opened the fridge and just stood still. Carter thought that he saw him physically shake.

"What the fuck…." Staff Green shouted. "What the fuck is this…?"

Carter smiled. "Mushrooms, Staff. I fancied some mushrooms earlier and must have forgotten to take them out," he said casually. In the fridge was a punnet of mushrooms that had been bought from the Naafi.

Staff Green didn't give him time to react; he just turned on the balls of his feet and hit Carter on the left side of his head. Carter took the full force just beside his bad eye and fell to the ground. His head felt like it had exploded as he lay on the floor looking up at Green's face red with rage. Suddenly it all came back to him. He remembered now that when he was getting ready to meet Lemska Green had barged into his room.

"Get the fuck up, you fucking shit Carter!"

Carter stayed on the floor. Green kicked him hard in the ribs. "I said get up!"

"I know what you fucking did, Green!" Carter screamed. "It was fucking you. You pushed me out of that fucking window."

"Look Carter, you are talking shit. No fucker did anything to you. You are just a soft cunt who can't handle it here."

"I know what you did, and I'll get you for it, you fucker!"

Green grabbed Carter around the neck and pulled his head to his. "Prove it!" Then he slammed Carter's head back to the floor, gave him another kick in the ribs and left the room.

Carter lay on the floor in agony.

***

"If it's true, there's fuck all you can do about it!" Barker stated.

"But he tried to kill me!"

"I would try to kill you if you shagged my wife."

Carter looked at Barker; there was no sympathy in his eyes. What he had just told him seemed to be like water off a duck's back. He had told him how it had been Staff Green who had thrown him out the window; that Staff Green had tried to kill him.

"I told you what this place is like. No one gives a shit. One of the lads here said he was going to commit suicide if they didn't post him out. Staff Green asked him how he planned to commit suicide. He said he was going to hang himself. Staff Green gave him a rope in the troop office in front of everyone. That night when everyone was down the bar the poor kid hung himself in the wash room. Wasn't found until six the next morning. What do you think happened?"

Carter stayed silent.

"Nothing, his body was shipped back to the UK and that was that."

"So you're telling me no one will care that Staff Green tried to kill me."

"Can you prove it?"

"No."

"Then if I was you I would keep your head down and try and get out of this place."

"That's it then?"

"Look Carter, you're not the most popular guy in the

Unit. No one really wants to be associated with you. No one gives a shit about you."

Carter lay in his bed as Toz, Lenny and Mark came into the room. They had three girls with them. Carter wasn't in the mood for this. He couldn't wait to get out on exercise.

He rolled over as the music came on; there was a giggle and a laugh and he heard Toz say, "Don't worry about him – he's gay!"

Chapter 18

Carter's life on exercise had been the usual hell, with no let up from Staff Green: litter picking, driving duties, peeling spuds, to the delight of Micky the cook and then on to the dishes. He was lucky to get any sleep! The only relief he got was the mid exercise break. He hadn't asked permission, but Tam had given him the rota for the time off and at the last minute he'd jumped into the back of the Land Rover where the lads were drinking beer, and was heading back to camp.

The driver was Jimmy, and when he saw two girls hitch-hiking he decided to pull over and ask them if they wanted a lift. They had looked at each other briefly before agreeing, then jumped in. They were both Dutch and on their way home from a music festival in Berlin. They readily accepted a beer, and after they'd had a few, agreed to lift their tops and show off their breasts. Before long Jonah's hands were all over one of the girls and one of the Line Men was having a good time with the other. The girls decided to come back to the barracks and Jonah took them both up to his room. They joined Jonah and Carter for the night, and in the morning Jonah and Carter were picked up by the Land Rover going back out to exercise. The girls were dropped off at the motorway junction.

"So Carter, what is this?" Staff Green looked at the paperwork on his desk

"I am requesting training with 264 for selection."

"And what says they will have you! I've already binned one application."

"You can't stop me - the padre said so."

"Oh yes I fucking can! Who the fuck is the padre to say what I can and can't do! I had that whinging Bible basher in here the other day talking about you. You found religion?" Green sneered.

Carter stayed silent.

"You still don't understand do you? The Army is about fitting in - not running off to some piss-head Bible basher who's here for God knows what." He paused. "You could probably piss all over 264 selection course. You could probably piss all over their technical assessments, but if you're a cunt, they won't want you. If *I* tell them you're a cunt, they won't want you."

'Just like Micky did to me here,' Carter thought to himself.

"The best thing for you, Carter, is to fucking go AWOL if you don't like it. That's the only way you'll ever get out of here." Staff Green smiled. "Now get down the garages and start sweeping, I will be inspecting in two hours."

***

"He said what? He was probably joking!" Carter stood in front of OC (Officer Commanding) of 1 Squadron.

"He said I would be better off going AWOL." Carter repeated. "And he meant it."

"I'm sure he was only jesting with you Corporal." The

OC looked at Carter's concerned face. "I will have a word with him."

***

"Request for training with 264 denied," Sergeant Bickerstaff stated.

"What?"

"Just had a letter through from manning and records; your request for training with 264 has been denied," and Bickerstaff looked up at Carter.

"Why would they deny training? I thought 264 were short of technicians?"

"Well, let's see what else comes up. You applied for 216, 13 Intelligence and the All Arms Commando Course, didn't you. They must be due in at any time."

"Fuck it! Why wouldn't they let me even try to pass the course?"

"Just sit it out! You'll be out of here before you know it."

"I'm really sick of all this shit I keep getting here. I'm in the cook house doing dish pan jobs, doing guard duties, doing silver service in the Officers' and Sergeants' Mess. I can't even get a move to TM Troop."

"Something will come up."

Carter turned and left the office close to tears.

Staff Green turned to Lieutenant Harrington, "So how long then before you reckon he'll go AWOL? I reckon by the end of the month."

"I'd have put money on it he'd have been gone by now! He's a stubborn little fucker."

"He's a muppet! He's like a dog with a rubber bone that keeps coming back for more."

"You've had him on solid ROPs for months now; up at

five parading and then mopping down the troop line stairs. He hasn't been out of barracks for all that time."

"Yep! And I think I'll step it up a bit more. Need to have a word with Toz. His life in that room is too comfortable!" Green smiled.

"You know Al, Carter isn't really too bad a lad. He's fit, smart, a good and pleasant soldier and - as you're aware! - takes orders. He's pretty much a model soldier."

"He's a cunt, and I will make him pay for being a cunt!" Green snapped.

Harrington was not going to argue with him. If he was determined to push Carter about, then there was nothing he was going to do to upset the apple cart. He had his second pip on his shoulder now, and it wouldn't be long before he was off to some new posting. His life here had been quiet, and he had never got involved with the day to day management of the lads. He left that to Staff Green and Sergeant Bickerstaff.

***

That night when Carter walked into his room he found his bed upended. The mattress was stuffed behind the frame, and the duvet and sheets were all in a crumpled pile. It was past midnight and Carter had just finished his ROP inspection. He had become immune by now to the shouting and the sarcasm, which in fact had got even worse in the last few weeks. The latest tactic was to have his boots stamped on by the Inspecting Sergeant, so he was forced to spend the night bulling them back to a shine ready for the next inspection.

Toz, Mark and Lenny were lying in their beds. Carter

196

said nothing, just pulled his bed frame back to the floor, re-made the bed and climbed in.

***

When Carter walked into his room the next night the bed frame stood on its end again, with the mattress was curled behind it, but this time there were no sheets or duvet. The window was open and Carter could see his bedclothes three floors below. It had been raining so the sheets and pillows were soaking. He went re-signedly down to collect them, and on the way back up he met Jonah just coming in.

Carter shook his head. "They're into trashing my bed every night now."

"Yes, Green really has it in for you. I've been told not to have you move rooms in any circumstances."

"What am I to do?"

"Sorry, mate! I've just got no idea."

Carter managed to hold back the tears, but his throat muscles tightened. This was a nightmare .He got to his room, and left the sodden sheets and pillow on the floor by his bed. He pulled the bed frame down and dragged the mattress onto it; then he got his sleeping bag out of his Bergen and climbed into it.

***

Carter sat in Lemska's living room with her father Heinrich. He had managed to get out of camp because the sergeant on duty that day did not want to both-er with ROPs. There was a European football match on, and he wanted to watch it and have a few beers in the Mess. He told Carter to go to his room, on no account to leave and to parade at 05:00hrs in his Number 2's. Carter had readily agreed, gone to his room and changed, and then jumped the fence at the back of the barracks.

They had been talking about the Army, with Heinrich saying he didn't get to speak much about his army days. Carter had thought that Heinrich had been a reluctant soldier, but as Heinrich explained; after the war everyone had been a reluctant soldier. In his youth, though, he could not wait to join up. He had joined the Army as soon as he could and had ended up in 2nd SS Panzer Division. His first stint with them had been on the Eastern Front. He had loved it, not many people in Germany are allowed to say that they loved being a soldier, but he did.

When the war was over he had to start from nothing and work his way up. A few in his company were from the original gang he formed after war, and had served with him. If anyone thought army life was tough, he said, they should have tried being in Germany at the end of the war trying to make something of yourself.

Carter found himself confiding that he was being bullied by a Staff Sergeant. Heinrich laughed. "Bullied are you? Are you soft? Our Lemska always likes the weak; she is always bringing them here like injured birds. She gets it from her mother - I am sure she does it on purpose to piss me off! When I was in," he boomed, "you had to fight each other all the time! In training we even had to fight over food. The one that won got to eat; the other went without, until he got to beat the other for food."

Carter didn't believe Heinrich, but went along with it.

"So what do you want to do, Chris?" Heinrich asked. "You volunteered to be in the Army, which is commendable, but now you don't like it because it's a bit hard for you and you're being picked on." Carter stayed silent.

"What would you do in business? If life got a bit hard, you didn't win a job, lost a bit of money. Would you cry? Would you give up?"

"No!"

"So why are you giving up now? You go back to your barracks, find this Staff Green and hurt him. Hurt him so he remembers being hurt. I have hurt people in my time, you know! And he smiled to himself.

"You see, Lemska has no worries about money. I have so much in her bank that even the most useless waif and stray could not deplete it. I have lawyers that will watch it, and what she does with it." Heinrich looked at Carter. "But you don't look like a waif and stray. You don't look like Lemska's sort. Yes, you have a fucked up face, but you're not a weak man. She likes weak men, or shall I say 'boys'.

Carter took a sip of his beer.

"You go now! Leave Lemska, and go and fight your fight. She will be bored with you in a few more weeks, leave as a strong man and let her have something to mope about. I like you Chris: this is why I say to you go, and have your fight and make it a good fight!"

Chapter 19

Carter sat on his bed, his roommates were asleep, Toz, Lenny and Mark were snoring away. They had not been disturbed when he had walked into the room. When he left Heinrich he had made up his mind that he would not see Lemska again. She was a nice girl but was a bit of a mother hen. Always fussing, always pulling his shirts down, worrying about how he looked, what he was thinking. If Carter told her what he was thinking now she would run a mile.

Carter had made up his mind; he was going to take the fight to them now. He was sick of his bed being wrecked, of the comments, not being able to make friends because everyone was now scared to be associated with him. How did his life end up in such a fucking mess?

Carter lay back on his bed and closed his eyes. Tomorrow would be a new dawn.

***

Carter got up early and started to have a shower before anyone else. He stood in the under the shower for ages, he could feel his heart beating in his chest as he thought about his next actions. He could feel his stomach knotting up in fear. He let the hot water sooth his head as his rage built up inside him. He stepped out the shower and stood in front of the mirror looking at his reflection as he brushed his teeth. His stomach was flat with his stomach muscles tight. His chest was muscled; there was no fat on him at all. He was a man of 20 and he was now ready to confront his tormentors.

The first into the showers was Lenny followed by Mark and Toz, Lenny bumped his shoulder into Carter who then turned and without warning smashed his fist into the side of Lenny's head sending Lenny sprawling into the tiled wall and then onto the floor. Lenny looked up at Carter holding onto his Jaw. "Oi you Cunt" Lenny was getting to his feet as Carter drove his bare foot up under Lenny's jaw sending his head smashing back into the tiled wall. This time Lenny didn't get back up.

Mark was first to react and drove his fist into Carter's lower back, then Toz was on him, smashing his fist into Carters stomach. As Carter leant forward, Mark smashed his knee into Carters face. Carter felt his nose explode in a flash of pain and heat. Then he felt another fist to the side of his head and he was on the ground. Mark stamped on his hand and Toz drove a fist into his side. Carter could not get up as he felt the blows reign down on him.

"You lot. stop! What the fuck are you lot up to?" Carter heard Jonah's voice.

"He fucking attacked Lenny, Man." Toz answered as he kicked Carter again. "The little queer shit."

"Cut it out Toz, get the fuck out of here." Jonah commanded. "Someone get Lenny up. Clear a space. Carter get to your feet."

"Jonah, he started it man. Look at Lenny, punched him in the face for no good reason."

"Fuck off Mark." Jonah snarled.

***

Carter had a light shone in his eye. "Follow the light" He did. "That's good. OK no concussion but your nose is broken. Nothing I can do there. Take these pain killers and keep out of trouble." The nurse smiled.

Carter dropped of the bed and took the pain killers she had offered him. He made his way out the medical center and back to the troop lines.

"Troop office!" Staff Green shouted as soon as he saw him.

Carter followed him into the office where he Green shut the door behind him. "OK Carter, I hear you had a bit of fun this morning, got yourself a bit of beating." Carter stayed silent.

"Try anymore of that fighting lark I will have you busted and put in jail for twenty eight days." Green looked at Carter. "Now get out of this office. That is another month of ROP's for you."

Carter did not go down stairs to the workshop. He went up to his room. He sat on his bed and started to cry.

***

Staff Green looked across at Toz. "The pushing is working. I want you to push some more. I want you to piss on his bed, smash some of his shit up."

"What about Jonah? They seem to be a bit gay for each other." Toz asked.

"Don't worry about Jonah, he has a promotion coming soon. He will be promoted to Sergeant and that'll mean he is moved out of the block. You my son, will be promoted to Corporal and you will take over Jonah's room and that of the position of troop lines corporal." Toz smiled. "When this happening then?"

"Within the month the promotions have been put forward and are just being processed with Manning and Records."

"Thanks Staff!" Toz stood and smiled.

***

"Think your fucking ard doing you sonny" Mark screamed in Carters face.

Lenny pushed him back on his bed. "Look what you did to my face you cunt." Lenny moaned at the big purple bruise that had formed on the side of this face. Carter had also dislodged Lenny's jaw bone which meant he would be struggling to eat for a while.

Toz walked up to Carters locker and undid his trousers and started to urinate in Carters locker.

"Oi! You twat." Carter screamed. Toz turned and smiled. Lenny and Mark pushed him to his bed and held him down. When Toz had finished urinating he grabbed the items Carter had on his shelf and knocked them to the floor.

"Now clean this shit up and get off and do your ROP's" Toz sneered.

Carter got up and looked into his locker. He grabbed all his clothes and put them on the bed. Taking them off the hangers he made his way out the room to take them to the washing machine.

***

Carter returned to his room at 12:30pm and found his bed soaked with urine. He lay on the floor near his bed with the smell urine in the air. He was not going to run.

***

The weeks passed. He had had a number of altercations with Toz, Mark and Lenny. He had attacked Lenny more than the other two and Lenny had started to back off. He would only mess Carter about if the other two were around and ready to defend him. He had tried to take Toz out but Toz had been too much for him and he had ended up losing badly.

Toz was now the troop lines Corporal, Jonah had been promoted to Sergeant and now lived in the Sergeants mess. Carter had not seen much of him lately. Lenny and Mark were not so forward in bothering Carter when they were alone; as Toz had his own room now, which also meant the parties had moved to Toz's room. Carter was left pretty much to himself, though they still trashed his bed and pissed on his duvet.

Carter had now got used to living like this. The main troop members had ostracized him. He still got on with Barker, but Barker was a law unto himself, but he was not going to be about forever. He had really taken the Wall Street bug and had now PVR'd himself, which had been unusually accepted on first request. Barker *did* have some influence somewhere.

One evening Jimmy invited Carter to have dinner with him and Suzy. Jimmy had invited him a few times when he had come out of hospital but he had turned him down as it was a bit of trek out to the married quarters. With all what was going on in camp it seemed like a good idea, get him out of barracks. Jimmy drove a small polo car and as they drove Jimmy was happily chirping away. Suzy was looking forward to meeting Carter again tonight, she had made her favourite soup and they had steak. How did he like his steak Jimmy had chirped away; what did he think of the Formula 1 championship. Should Prost have taken the championship from Senna? Now that was a battle between team mates. What was going on in Russia? Was communism over? Was the Berlin wall going to come down? And on he chirped.

They had pulled up in the married quarters, four tall blocks of flats in a semi-circle, surrounded by local German flats. Jimmy parked the car and they caught the lift to the eight floor. Jimmy opened the door to the flat and they walked in.

The flat was nice and warm, with warm lighting a leather sofa and cream carpets. Carter walked into the living room and sat down, he suddenly noticed Suzy in the open plan kitchen in a red camisole. It was skin tight from what he could see over the work top.

"Hi Chris" Suzy smiled.

"Hi Suzy" Chris answered back.

"Do want a beer Chris?" Jimmy asked as he went over to the fridge giving Suzy a peck on the cheek as he went to the fridge.

"Beer would be good." Carter said. He felt guilty looking Suzy's shape, but it seemed to be a game between these two. Jimmy came over with two bottles of beer and handed one to Carter and then went and sat on the single chair leaving Carter to sit on the sofa. Suzy walked into the living room her camisole was short and left nothing to the imagination. Carter could see her red coloured nickers and her naked breasts through the red material. He felt his penis stiffen as Suzy came and sat next to him. She smelt sexy and clean. Carter did not know what to do. He sat and drank his beer and Suzy crossed her legs beside him and put her hand on his thigh.

"So how are you feeling now Chris? Have you got better?"

"Yeah, it is like it never happened, it just this eye that never righted itself."

"Ah, that is sad, you had such a pretty face, but not that this scar changes anything, makes you look more rugged." Suzy purred. Carter turned to Jimmy who just sat back and watched with a smile on his face.

"Thank you, Suzy. I have got used to it now. Don't really notice it now."

Suzy smiled at him and turned to Jimmy. "You want to put some music on or is there some football you boys would like to watch?" Suzy asked. She got back up and went into the kitchen. "Do you boys want another beer? Food will be ready in a moment."

Carter watched as Suzy bent down to get the food out of the oven, he breasts came into full view as the camisole hung from her chest. Carter turned to Jimmy who just smiled at him. Carter did not know what to do, he felt uncomfortable. This was different from the hospital, in the hospital it had seemed like harmless fun looking at Suzy's breasts, now it seemed a little perverse.

"I'll put some sounds on." Jimmy got up and put the hi-fi six cd changer on random. The first track to play was a James Brown song. "So; how you getting on in the Squadron Chris?" Jimmy asked. "Looks like Staff Green's still got in for you. Rumour is that you were having it off with his wife."

"That's just rumours Jimmy, you know how it is!"

"Well if you were, you're a lucky man, she was fit looking girl." Jimmy smiled. "Not so fit when we had to go and pick her up though. Green had done a right number on her. Her face was a bit of a mess."

"He is just a bully." Carter stated.

"Yeah, but some blokes don't like their wives being touched by other men."

"Wasn't my fault." Carter pleaded his innocence. "She came on to me."

"Did you here that Suzy?" Jimmy shouted over to Suzy. "Chris here could not help himself, she came on to him." Jimmy smiled at Carter.

"Really…. That is interesting." Suzy smiled back at Jimmy.

Suzy prepared the food on plates then placed them on a small round table in the kitchen area. "Come on boys, food is ready." Suzy stated.

Jimmy and Carter got up and went to the table. Suzy and Jimmy sat opposite and Carter in the middle of the two around a round table. Suzy had made a Goulash and Mash and it tasted great. Carter complimented her on the food. They had a sweet German wine with the food. Jimmy stated how he liked to drink beer but liked to have wine with meals.

They talked generally about, the soviet bloc, was the

wall coming down, was there going to be an eastern bloc war or would it end up in the Middle East. Then they began to talk about the camp, life in general, the exercises, the army and was it worth staying in. Jimmy and Suzy came from Middlesbrough, that they had been school sweethearts and had married as soon as Jimmy had his first posting. He had been in the Army ten years and loved it. It gave him a house, a job and some money in his pocket and he got to go to places he would never have gone if he had stayed in Middlesbrough plus Suzy did not have to work and life was good.

Carter had said, he wished it had gone a bit smoother when he had arrived, that if he could turn back time or had got a different posting. It had all gone wrong on the first day and the little shit 'Micky' talking shit before he got there.

"You're among good friends here." Suzy touched his leg under the table.

"Yes good friends, Chris." Jimmy and Suzy raised their glasses which Carter joined. "Cheers."

They finished the meal, and Suzy asked if they wanted desert, in which they both said 'yes' to and she brought out some slices of Black Forest Gateau. They had some more wine and Carter was beginning to relax, Jimmy was smiling and talking a lot, telling jokes and being rather jovial, Suzy laughed and this became infectious and Carter laughed also. Jimmy was a funny little man, with his skinny little body and his thin moustache from the 1950's.

"Shall we go and sit back on the soft chairs?" Jimmy asked.

"Go on boys, I will clear up here."

"Fancy something stronger?" Jimmy asked. "I have a nice whiskey, Talisker, a real peaty one from the West Coast. I was up there doing some climbing exercises a few years ago. Loved it; got to drink this with some of the locals."

"Go on then." Carter said.

Suzy was in the kitchen clearing plates away, and doing the dishes. She seemed to be busying herself. 'Nothing Compares to You' by Sinead O'Connor came on the hi-fi. "I like this song, but she is a supporter of the IRA. BFBS have banned playing the song." Jimmy said. "Shame, funny old world we live in. Why people want to fight about nothing really. But I suppose it keeps us in a job."

"It would be a better world if everyone just got on and was happy" Suzy said as she made her way back into the living room. She climbed on the sofa next to Carter pulling both of legs up and leaning forward so both her large breast were squeezed between her arms.

Carter could not help but feel uncomfortable; he felt heat in his cheeks. Suzy put her arm on his leg and smiled. "What are you Carter; are you a fighter?"

"Well I thought I was a bit of a fighter." Carter looked at Suzy's breasts.

"Oi, I bet you are. You have very muscly legs; I bet you are all muscle." Suzy smiled.

Carter turned to look a Jimmy who was sipping his whisky smiling.

"You know, Chris, you can have her." Jimmy said matter of factly.

"What." Chris gasped.

"You can fuck her if you want Chris, I don't mind. I like to watch."

"I...I... can't Jimmy." Chris said. "You have been so kind to me and....."

"Don't worry Chris, it's just fucking. We have been married since we was eighteen. It has been ten years. Suzy likes a bit of a change every now and then and I don't mind as long as I know."

"Come on Chris, I bet you know how to treat a woman." Suzy purred.

"I am sorry I can't." Chris moaned as he looked at Suzy. "I can't."

"But you fucked Ingrid." Suzy moaned.

"It was different."

"If you want, you can take me into the bedroom. Jimmy won't mind."

"No, I know. I just don't feel right."

Suzy dropped her top off her shoulders so her breasts were free and grabbed Carters hand. "Feel me, touch me. You can do what you want with me" She purred.

Carter stood, and turned to both of them. "I am sorry, but I can't. It is not you Suzy, you are beautiful, but I just can't."

Suzy looked at Jimmy and then they both looked at Carter. "That's ok Chris. Anytime you change your mind, feel free to come and visit."

Suzy got up from the sofa letting her camisole fall to the ground so she stood there in just her knickers. She pecked Carter on the cheek, "Think about it Chris and come back when you are ready."

Carter thanked them for dinner and the drinks and excused himself and left. He could feel his cock hard in his trousers. 'That was serial' he thought to himself. 'Was anyone normal in this place?'

As he got out into the cold night, he wondered how he was going to get back to barracks. It was past nine and it was a good six mile walk back to barracks. As he set his mind to do the walk, a car bibbed him from behind. He turned to see Tam at the wheel of a Ford Escort. "What you doing around here, Chris?" Tam Asked from the driver's seat.

"Just had dinner at Jimmies." Carter stated.

"Oh, Yeah, have you now." Tam smiled. "Well where you off to now?"

"Back to barracks."

"Well why don't you jump in and come around for a few beers. Jonah is up at the flat keeping the little one occupied on the Amiga."

Carter nodded and jumped in the passenger seat. They made their way to a local supermarket and bought three Herfy handbags, Tam also bought himself forty cigarettes. They then made their way back to the flats. Tam lived in a block two away from where Jimmy lived. When they got to the Tam's front door, he let himself in and called out. "Look who I found skulking about." Chris walked in behind him and said Hello to Tams wife Tracy. Jonah was at the Amiga 500 with a small child who was jumping up and down on his knees beside Jonah in excitement.

"Tracy, take some of the beers." Tam said, "Chris, come through and take a pew."

Chris took a seat on the sofa; it was a green leather sofa with solid decorated wood arms, all the fashion in Germany. Chris relaxed as he watched Jonah play on the Amiga 500, Tam and Tracy sat on the same chair, the TV showing a drama on BFBS TV. This was a family house.

"Tommy, you're going to have to go to bed soon." Tracy said to the small boy.

"Ahhh... why?" The child moaned.

"You have school in the morning and it is coming up to half nine, way past your bed time young man."

"Ahhh...."

"Get too it, teeth and jim jams."

Carter relaxed on the sofa watching Jonah play Kick off 2 on the Amiga 500.

After fifteen minutes and a good night from Tommy, Tam, Carter and Jonah settled down to play the football game on the Amiga while Tracy watched the TV."

"So what were you doing out here Chris?" Jonah asked.

"I was having dinner with Jimmy." Jonah raised an eye brow and Tam smiled.

"Yeah, ok."

"Seriously I was, why?"

"You don't know?" Tam asked suspiciously.

"Know, what?" Carter asked.

"They are part of the wife swapping circle around here. There's a whole bunch of them that have sex parties and the likes. Dress the men up in sheets so the women cannot see their faces and only have one hole if you know what I mean."

"Nah, you joking." Carter tried to feign surprise.

"You telling me that Jimmy did ask you to shag his wife while he watched...."

"Oi would you lot shut up, I am trying to watch the telly." Tracy moaned.

"No how do you know any how?" Carter asked.

"Common knowledge, half the bleeding pads are in on it." Tam said.

"What, you as well?" Carter asked Tam.

"Nah." Tam laughed. "Me and the Mrs are too ugly!"

"Talk for yourself, bug eyes." Tracy laughed.

Carter went red. "Ah no worries with Tracy. We are just normal, the others are just a bit all messed in the head. Here have another beer and you can play the winner."

For the next hour or two they played the game, Tracy got up and went to bed leaving the boys engrossed in their game.

"So, Chris, Did your little outburst sort everything out the other morning."

"Nah." Carter stated. "Tell you the truth, to me it is just the norm. Not so bad that Toz has his own room now. Mark and Lenny are not so tough when he's not about, plus the parties have moved to Toz's room."

"You do get a bit messed about sonny." Tam said. "But I would not worry too much, these things pass. I remember when I was in the Falklands, pissed out of my head, 25th birthday it was. They came out with a special cake, all candles and the likes. I ate the lot, told everyone they were not having a piece. It was shite, mate. They had made me a shite cake, covered it in cream and I ate it; didn't live it down for ages."

"There was that other guy, he was a Tech. He was down in the Falklands, as a joke, wrote a letter to his mate's wife pretending it was him, said he was having an affair; that he wanted a divorce had been done for D & D and all sorts of shit. The wife went to the padre with this letter, grief stricken and they were both shipped home. The guy got shit for that for ages."

"What we're saying is, shit will pass. A new tech will come in and you will be forgotten about. Just knuckle in let time pass you by."

"But he did shag Staff Green wife." Jonah stated.

"Yeah, there is that factor." Tam and Jonah both laughed.

**

The next morning Carter was awoken by Jonah. They had stayed over at Tam's in the spare room after going to bed about two in the morning. Carters head was throbbing. Tracy was up and making coffee and toast. "Morning Chris, looks like you are part of the gang now." Tam smiled. "Get some food down you and you two; be off with you."

They drove back to barracks in Jonah's Vauxhall Astra GTE. Jonah was so pleased with his electronic display; it was like something out of Knight Rider. Jonah raced the car as fast the engine would let him back to the barracks. Once there, Jonah dropped Carter off at his barrack block before going off to the Sergeants Mess. Carter made his way up to his room, and to his surprise his bed was in tack and nothing had been disturbed. He stripped down grabbed his towel and went off to the showers.

Chapter 20

The air was crisp, it was not far past 9am and the sun had yet to melt the frost off the ground. Carter was in the first shooting detail. The ammo boxes had been opened and the brass glinted in the sun.

"Take 3 mags worth, a ten and two twenties." The shooting detail was instructed.

Carter put his hand into the box containing the 7.62mm round and pulled a handful out and put them in his combat jacket pocket. No one looked at him and he knew what he was doing, he knew that he had more than fifty rounds on him when he walked away from the table. He loaded his three magazines with a ten and two twenties. The remaining rounds he tucked into the bottom of his day sack. He counted eighteen rounds.

Carter did his shoot, scored marksman, knowing he would get no praise from Staff Green at any point. Members for the squadron shooting team were to be selected today for Bisley shooting team, Carter knew that he would be left off the list. He was one of the best shots in the squadron, outscored Staff Green on most shoots now. The was no way Staff Green was going to let him get on the shooting team; let him have an easy life spending day after day at the ranges for a couple of months training before then going on a jolly for a week in England for the competition itself.

After what happened at Christmas Carter knew he was stuck here. His life was to be a misery until his four years was up; there was no way he was being posted out, he would be blocked on every move. He had been told by the nurse that he was supposed to have been posted out after the accident, but Staff Green had blocked it. 'Accident' everyone called it an 'Accident' Staff Green had tried to murder him, but he had no proof and no-one would believe him even if he did tell someone.

Well he had decided what he would do something about it now.

Carter sat in his usual spot on the ranges in the butts watching the targets being raised and lowered, scored, patched up and raised again. This went on all day. He no longer messed about with the scores. The poor shooters took three of four attempts to scrape a pass.

At the end of the day, everyone was lined up and declared "I have no live rounds or empty shells on my possession, Sir!" Carter knowing he had eighteen rounds in his day sack, but no one ever checked.

On getting back to camp, Carter cleaned his weapon; he never went up in the first group to have his weapon inspected for cleanliness by Staff Green as he knew he would be sent back to clean it again. He cleaned it, waited to the end when the last of the soldiers had finished theirs before taking it up to get it signed back into the armoury. Staff Green would always pick something up, call him a 'cunt' make him do some press ups before accepting the rifle on the second inspection. Carter and the troop had got used to this routine. The weaker of the lads in the troop were happy to have Carter in the troop as he took a lot of the attention they would normally receive off them.

Now Staff Green had been living in the Sergeants Mess for a few months he had now taken the bullying of Carter a little further. He now had a tendency to visit Toz in the troop lines. He had started to join in the parties that Toz had in his room, and Staff Green and Toz had started drinking together a lot more. No matter who Carter turned to, no one would help him. Jonah, Tam, Barker all told him it would pass. It did not pass, Carters bed was being trashed regularly, pissed on, his locker trashed and his clothes damaged. He could not have anything of his own out. His hi-fi had gone out the window. He had had a private word with his troop officer and then the squadron commander but both had fobbed him off. No one would let him change troops or be posted out. It was as if they wanted him to go AWOL. If he did that he would end up in the Military Corrective Training Centre in Colchester and he didn't want that. He was not going to go AWOL he was going to sort this out himself.

He buried the rounds on the perimeter fence line when he had been on a guard duty. There was no way he could keep them in his room with the constant attacks his kit had and he could not tell anyone he had them. He knew when he was going to use them. There was a combat exercise coming up. For two weeks of the year the Regiment when on an infantry training exercise. They played soldier in battle groups, marched around attacking each other's positions, did weapon training and had classes from other Regiments on tactics, and other training, the best bit was when a SAS instructor came and did some field training. It was fun; it was a bit of soldiering. It was also a time when you could take some of your aggression out on people you did not like. Carter smiled as he remembered basic training. They had been doing an exercise of over running a position. Pepper Potting into an enemy line, over running it. He had then ordered and all round defence while he and one other had gone back to check the dead on the position they had just over run. It was a standard drill; treat a dead body as a live one until you were sure. The DS had been playing the enemy and one corporal had played Carter up a bit in training. He dropped hard on the back of his legs with his knees, punched the corporal in the ribs, and then held him by the shoulders as he rolled him to his side. A thunder flash went off and the drill was over. Carter scored full marks for the correct drills but the corporal said he would get him back for the slapping, which he did at the end of training party, where Carter was punched a few times for being a cocky twat by the Corporal.

The build up to the war games was a number of lessons in camp on first aid, map reading, field craft and survival, Nuclear Biological and Chemical Warfare drills (NBC). Why this consisted of running around camp with a telegraph pole on your shoulders in full NBC kit and respirator Carter could never work out.

A few days before the battle camp started the exercise build up started to appear on orders. There was a story around the battle camp. An East German Army unit had gone and downed arms and crossed the border, was the first bit of news. The western governments had given this East German Unit sanctuary which had resulted in another East German Army unit crossing the border. The Russian government had requested the repatriation of these two units, which the western governments denied. The Russians now did a show of force and had moved a large contingent of troops onto the border.

The exercise had been given the name 'Operation Safe Guard' and it was about to be put into action. The last details on squadron orders is that there had been a small fire fight between a border patrol and the Russian troops on the border just south of Berlin. Tensions were escalating.

Chapter 21

Suddenly the door burst open, the lights came on. Toz was at the door. "Get up Boys, we off to play soldiers!" Carter turned to look at his clock. It was just past 2 am. Lenny and Mark were up and the corridor was full of activity. There was time to grab a quick shower and a shave. Within twenty minutes Carter was heading to the square where the Regiment was separating itself into its units and the awaiting Four- Tonners. The parade square was full of activity; the later arrivals were the soldiers from the married quarters as they had to travel in. Within forty five minutes the wagons were fired up and heading out of camp. Each section had been given its orders. There had been an invasion in force of Russian troops across the border. The enemy troops were being played by the Black Watch. They never played nicely and if you got caught up with them. Everyone was in the back of the Four-Tonner, cammed up with SLR's and all carrying blanks. The Four-Tonner bounced along, a few people were smoking, most had their eyes closed getting some more sleep. Staff Green was in the back of the Four-Tonner next to Toz and Lenny. They were in conversation looking over to Carter every now and again, smiling. Carter smiled to himself, he was ready now to make his move,

Staff Green would feel the pain and it would teach him that you could not get through life being a bully. The Four-Tonner bounced along for another hour before pulling up sharply, the rear tail gate was kicked open and everyone jumped off the back. It was still dark and everyone was called to form up into ranks.

The Major of the squadron stood at the front and gave a quick briefing.

"Ok Lads, we have now been put on the ground to protect this area. There has been a build-up of Russian Troops North of here and our job is to hold the line and prevent them from crossing further into West Germany." He paused. A number of soldiers looked bored, they had done this a number of times before and all they could think of was two weeks of tabbing, dummy fights and if they got caught, and you always did; a few days of interrogation training. Shit this was probably what they had joined up for but after a number of years sitting in the backs of wagons drinking tea, this was the last thing they wanted to be doing. "Right, officers and Senior NCO's on me for further briefing. Men, get you kit together and have a smoke before we head off and go hard tack."

Carter looked about and went over to join Barker who was setting up his small gas burner to make a coffee. He pulled a book out of his webbing. Carter smiled. It was a beginner's guide to the Stock Market. "You're really going for it then?"

"I tell you, if someone had told me about this game before I joined up I wouldn't have bothered."

"Well I am sure it's not that easy, otherwise everyone would be at it."

"The clever people are."

"Well how long you got before you're out?"

"Eleven months and counting." Barker smiled.

"You want some of this hot water?"

Carter nodded and sat down with Barker and they had a coffee.

After about ten minutes, Staff Green and Lieutenant Harrington came back to the group.

"OK men. Listen up!" Staff Green growled.

Lieutenant Harrington paused before saying. "Ok we are breaking up into our troops. Panther troop circulate on me. Everyone else, fuck off and find your troop commanders."

There was a movement of people before only Panther troop stood in front of Lieutenant Harrington.

Carter smiled back and then looked at Lieutenant Harrington.

"OK, we are to move out and move to a position eight clicks from here. There we are to hold position and observe the area for hostiles. We are not to engage with hostiles only observe; any questions?"

"What if we are engaged by Hostiles? Can we fire back?" Peterson asked getting into the spirit of the game.

"Good question, Peterson." Harrington smiled. "If we are engaged then we will make the call at them time."

Carter smiled. They were not going to be engaged, this was all part of the war games. Everything was a drill and a test. An 8km march with full kit just happened to be part of a combat test. The next would be set up a position with all round defence and sometime during the next 24 hours this would be tested.

The troop packed away their kit and put their Bergen's on their backs. Most were carrying about 60 pounds in their packs and about 30 pounds in the webbing. The troop set off at a marching pace in two columns. Carter was in the middle of the group. The tab lasted just under two hours. They tabbed into a wooded area and as far as Carter could see they were now in a military exercise area. They entered a wood and from the look of the ground a number of shell scraps had been dug and filled in, so this location had been used a number of times.

The troop was told to form into all round defence. The corporals were given six men each to be their section. Carter ended up being part of Toz's section. Toz at the time was enjoying his role as section commander and forgot about Carter. He had Lenny and Mark close. Carter was pretty much on his own as no one in the section really had much to do with him. He took up his position in the all-round defence. Set up is arcs and dug his shell scrape. This would be it for the next few hours. Once he dug his shell scape and he made himself a brew and waited for the next order.

In the next ten minutes the guard roster was sent around. Carter was not due on guard for a few hours. This was the army; hurry up and wait. Carter lay in his shell scrape with his SLR rifle looking out into the wilderness in front of him.

**

It was around mid-night, the section had been in the same location for the day and into the night. Carter was on guard with Peterson who was just about to finish he hour. Carter told him to put his head down and he would find Smudge who was next up for stag. Carter heard Peterson settle into his basher but did not go and find Smudge to wake him for his guard duty. He sat, waited and listened for everything to be calm. The troop was all asleep in their sleeping bags in their bashers.

Carter took a magazine out of his webbing and looked at the live ammo he had in it. He smiled to himself and then got up. Looked about again, listened, there was no movement, some snoring but no movement.

Carter made his way over to the basher where Staff Green lay asleep. He stood over it, undid the cord from the tree and pulled the basher away so he could see Staff Greens face. He raised his SLR and drove it into Staff Greens face. He did not care if he had killed him, he leant down and picked the lifeless body of Staff Green up and threw him over his shoulder. He then made his way out of the troop defence lines into the night.

***

The sun had risen and the crisp air hurt on the face. Carter sat in the crater he had found and watched for any life from Staff Green. He knew he was breathing, he had checked that a while ago. The blow to the head had knocked Staff Green un-conscious.

He looked over the lip of the crater and was happy with his location. He was in the middle of a plain and had visibility of at least a kilometre around him and the ground was flat. He could have not wished for better.

He pulled his flask out of his webbing and had a drink, and then opened a chocolate bar from his ration pack.

He sat back and looked up into the now blue sky.

***

Staff Green opened his eyes slowly, his head hurt like hell. He could see Carter sitting drinking from his mug and they were in what looked like a crater and not the troop lines.

"What the fuck?" Staff Green said.

***

Carter smiled at Staff Green and pulled his rifle to his shoulder and shot Staff Green in the right knee.

***

Staff Green, screamed as he felt his leg explode at the knee.

***

"Now Staff Green" Carter said. "That is your career over. There is no fucking way they are going to put that knee back together."

***

Sergeant Bickerstaff and Lieutenant Harrington stood with each other looking at the men formed up in a squad. "Well where the fuck could those to have gone." Lieutenant Harrington asked. "It's been two fucking hours. I am going to call this in."

Sergeant Bickerstaff shrugged his shoulders. He had torn into Toz in the morning when he realised that there was no guard out, then they had found that Staff Green and Carter were missing.

"Radio Operator. Call Stingray and call an end to this exercise. We have two men missing." Lieutenant Harrington shouted.

The troop looked at each other not knowing what to think or say.

***

Carter threw Staff Green a bandage and told him to put a tourniquet on his leg as there was no-one coming to save him for a while and he needed to stop the bleeding.

"What the fuck, Carter, have you lost your mind?" Staff Green shouted.

"That's what you wanted wasn't it Al? Can I call you Al? Of course I can."

"Carter what is this, you've fucking shot me."

"And you tried to fucking kill me, tick for tack." Carter smiled.

"Look Carter, lets sort this out!" Staff Green pleaded.

"There was plenty of time for that, you could have posted me, let me be, but no, you wanted to push it." Carter said. "Now I want to push it. How much pain can I put you through before either; one they find us, or two, you die." Carter then raised his rifle again and shot Staff Green in the elbow. "What do you think Al, do you think they will get here in time."

***

Lieutenant Harrington stood in front of the Squadron Commander in the Command tent. "What do you mean, you have two men missing, we have only been out in the field less than 24 hours?"

"The troop found them missing this morning." Lieutenant Harrington explained.

"Who are these missing men?" The Squadron Commander asked.

"Staff Green and Corporal Carter."

"Corporal Carter, he is the chap that wanted posting out, the guy that fell out the window?"

"Yes Sir."

"OK, let's get a helicopter called in and do an aerial search." The Squadron Commander shook his head.

***

"You should have just let me be." Carter moaned.

"What was I supposed to do? Run."

"Yes, you were supposed to fucking run."

"But why? Why did you hate me so much?"

"Because I could, I have the power to do what I want here. I had everything I needed, you changed that, you shagged my wife."

"Your wife shagged anything, you would have found out at some point." Carter moaned.

"But I found out it was you." Staff Green sighed, "I think I could have handled it better if it had been any-one but you"

Carter picked up his rifle again.

"Stop, no, enough, don't shoot me anymore." Staff Green begged.

"Now you know what it's like" Carter smiled as he fired another round into Staff Greens good knee.

Staff Green screamed.

"Use the tourniquet between legs, you know the drill." Carter said matter of factly.

Above Carter heard the rota's of a Gazelle Helicopter, as it came closer Carter raised his weapon and fired a round at the underbelly. The helicopter engine screamed as the pilot turned to the left and banked heavily before flying off.

***

"What do you mean they took live fire." The Squadron Commander said to the Radio Operator.

"That's what they said." The radio operator stated. "They took live fire from this grid reference. There were two figures in an artillery shell crater and one of the figures fired a live round at the under belly of the aircraft and hit it. They said it was some good shooting who ever took the pot shot. They ain't happy bunnies." The radio operator smiled.

"Get on to the Military Police. I also want this unit at that location and let's see what the is going on"

***

Carter could see the troops in the distance. He lay in the prone position and waited for them to get to about 600 meters. He then fired off two rounds above their heads. He smiled as he watch them dive for cover.

He then turned to Staff Green who was becoming pale.

"Remember the Tourniquet Al" Carter smiled.

Staff Green looked at Carter but did not say anything, blood was soaking into the ground all around him.

***

Lieutenant Harrington lay beside the Squadron Commander. "Where the hell did that man get live rounds from Lieutenant?" The Squadron Commander asked.

"No idea Sir."

Sergeant Bickerstaff turned to Jonah, "I knew this was going to end in tears. Did you know anything about this?"

Jonah turned to Sergeant Bickerstaff, "Had no idea. I know he was being messed about, but I didn't know he was about to lose it."

"Fuck, this is going to be messy" Sergeant Bickerstaff moaned.

***

"Don't worry Al, they are nearly here for you." Carter smiled as he kicked Staff Green so he did not pass out.

***

The Squadron Commander now had a loud hailer. "Carter. Can you hear me Carter.? I would like to speak to you."

***

"Did you hear that Al, they want to talk to me now." Carter said to Staff Green. "And you know what. I am going to talk to them."

He raised his Rifle and placed a white handkerchief on it and waived it above the Crater lip.

***

"Sir someone seems to be waiving a white flag." Lieutenant Harrington told the Squadron Commanding Officer.

"If that is you Carter, throw the weapon to the ground and walk towards us with your hands up!" The Squadron Commander ordered into the loud hailer.

***

"That's it Al, all over. I am now going to hand myself in now, what do you think about that Al? and what do you think I will get?" Carter said to the half-conscious Staff Green. "A few years in jail, I haven't killed you, when this goes to court all the shit of this place will come out. I'll do less time than I signed up for."
Carter smiled at Staff Green. "And you thought you'd fuck me up. Look at you now Al. Who's the one all fucked up!!"
Carter stood up with hands up and made his way out of the crater.

The End

More Great Exciting Fast Paced Novels by Percy Publishing:

Sabre Six : File 51 by Jamie Fineran

Michael Fox is on the way home to his wife and daughter after saving the life of a French Industrialists son.

On the way through Paris De Nord station about to catch the Eurostar he is propositioned by Stan an Ex-colleague from the SAS who now works for MI5.

Michael is to follow Ryan Killeen into London and report where he goes once he leaves the train.

Michael's life will never be the same after he accepts the simple task for £10,000.

"For Fans of Fast Paced Action Thrillers" Soldier Magazine.
"Fantastic Debut Novel" Phil Campion.
"A Must Read" Airsoft Magazine.

ISBN 978-0-9571568-3-8

Ace of Spades : File 52 by Jamie Fineran

The year is 2015 and the Coalition Forces are pulling out of Afghanistan, leaving MI5 boss Stan to an embarrassing and delicate situation.

His perfect soldier with the impeccable 22 year Army record has gone rogue, taking Merlin Security with him - the very security assigned to safeguard the one thing the British Government needs.

Two mercenaries are deployed to restore Government control. It's a deceptively simple, but potentially deadly mission.

So who IS in control of the poppy fields?

ISBN : 978-0-9571568-6-9

Unsceptred Isle : Three of a Kind by Joseph V Sultana

Society has gone to hell.

And as the collapse spreads, Jon Maitland is building a wall.

A wall that costs him his family.

As the world implodes, Baker has become abandoned and lost in this new world.

Ridiculed and outcast in his youth, Latimer is now the lunatic in charge of this asylum known as Launceston.

Maitland needs out.

Baker Wants Out.

Does Latimer hold the Key to the Unsceptred Isle?

ISBN 978-0-9571568-0-7

PERCY
PUBLISHING

Visit www.percy-publishing.com for more information.

Facebook: www.facebook.com/percypublishing

Twitter: @percypublishing

To Contact John Marsh Find him on FaceBook
https://www.facebook.com/john.marsh.3576224